THE BRICK MAN 2

Lock Down Publications and Ca$h Presents

THE BRICK MAN 2

A Novel by *King Rio*

Lock Down Publications
P.O. Box 944
Stockbridge, Ga 30281
www.lockdownpublications.com

First Edition November 2021
Printed in the United States of America

Lock Down Publications
Like our page on Facebook: Lock Down Publications @ www.facebook.com/lockdownpublications.ldp
Book interior design by: **Shawn Walker**

Stay Connected with Us!

Text **LOCKDOWN** to 22828 to stay up-to-date with new releases, sneak peaks, contests and more…

Thank you!

Submission Guideline.

Submit the first three chapters of your completed manuscript to ldpsubmissions@gmail.com, subject line: Your book's title. The manuscript must be in a .doc file and sent as an attachment. Document should be in Times New Roman, double spaced and in size 12 font. Also, provide your synopsis and full contact information. If sending multiple submissions, they must each be in a separate email.

Have a story but no way to send it electronically? You can still submit to LDP/Ca$h Presents. Send in the first three chapters, written or typed, of your completed manuscript to:

LDP: Submissions Dept
P.O. Box 944
Stockbridge, Ga 30281

DO NOT send original manuscript. Must be a duplicate.

Provide your synopsis and a cover letter containing your full contact information.

Thanks for considering LDP and Ca$h Presents.

Dedication

Dedicated to my nephew Justin Jr. Welcome to the world. Uncle Mario loves you!

This one is strictly for the readers, the new ones and the ones of old, those who've been with me since The Cocaine Princess was released in February of 2013 and those who've just heard of me. I hope you all enjoy this read. The first three books in this series were some of the last books I typed up myself, sitting alone in a segregation cell with nothing but a smartphone and my burgeoning literary thoughts. I was able to do all the necessary research and see all the people who inspired those characters I first introduced in The Ring series years ago. Now that series has been republished under Lock-down Publications as Mobbed Up, and I'm just about done writing part 5! Parts 1 through 5 of The Brick Man series are already complete as well, so be prepared for the next novel in this series, because it's on the way.

Once again, I wouldn't be releasing any of these titles without Ca$h, so shout out to the big homie and the entire LDP roster. Shout out to my sisters Mariah, Shakia, Tanisha, and Ne-Ne, my brothers Will, Kenneth, Marcus, and Bodie, and to all those glorious Earls and Bardletts in Chicago and elsewhere that have shown their love and support throughout the past sixteen years of missed opportunities. Pretty sure I'll be seeing you all next year! ;)

As always, Undying Love to all the readers and all the bruddas on lock. Mighty on that! (Inside talk lol.)

Contact me on FB: Author Rio

Instagram:@authorrio5

Email: authorrio@gmail.com

Or send mail to:

Mario Bardlette #120178

21390 Old State Road 37

Branchville, IN 47514

Prologue:

Scandal in Chiraq

August 26, 2016

Tamia was half asleep when she suddenly felt Kobe's hands slip behind her knees and push her legs up into the air. She kept her eyes shut and took a deep, relaxing breath, readying herself for the rough vaginal pounding that was sure to follow. Kobe had moved in with her almost two months ago, mere days after his ex-girlfriend Shawnna broke up with him, and since then she'd grown used to the predawn sex sessions. He had a habit of waking up with an erection, rolling over on top of her, and fucking her senseless.

But this time there was something different.

She felt the warmth of his breath on her pussy. Then came the feel of his tongue and lips on her clitoris, which Tamia found utterly surprising; Kobe had never put his mouth anywhere near her pussy. He always said that pussy-eating was for lesbians, that real niggas didn't eat pussy.

So what was it that had changed his mind? Was it because he was tired of hearing her complain about his two friends – Darren, a scrawny-built teenager with a long mop of dread-locks on his head, and the foul-mouthed thirteen-year-old RoRo-G – who'd been essentially living in the living room of her apartment for the past three weeks? Was it because tomorrow was her birthday?

She cast aside the questions as the tip of his tongue began probing her asshole and for five whole seconds she didn't breathe. She'd always wondered if it would feel good to get her assholelicked. It really did. She didn't want him to stop. Ever.

She tried holding in the moans but a moment later they escaped her lips, making it apparent that she was now fully awake. Keeping her eyes closed, she pulled the pillow from behind her head and, using both hands, pressed it to her face. "Yes. Don't stop. Please," she said into the pillow, moaning and panting between every word.

Tamia's nipples were hard and her body was tingling. The hand holding her left knee traveled down the underside of her thigh as the tongue made its much-anticipated return to her clitoris. A finger slipped into her asshole. She rolled her hips and shouted a stream of expletives into the pillow.

"Oh, fuck… Oh, fuck… Oh, shit… Mmm, oh, my God, I'm coming!"

She flung the pillow off of her face and looked down as the climax seized her only to find that it was not her handsome boyfriend Kobe's head between her thighs. It was his friend Darren.

Tamia laughed and gasped and slapped Darren upside the head, but she made no move to stop him from lapping up her orgasmic juices. Her eyes darted around the neatly organized bedroom, stopping first on the digital clock on her bedside table, then moving to the open closet door and the closed bedroom door.

It was 9:48 A.M.

"You asshole," Tamia said, scooting back toward the headboard. She got off of the bed, picked up a pair of small cotton shorts and a t-shirt from a chair in the corner, and put them on. "Where in the hell is Kobe? I know he put you up to this shit."

"Nah, no he didn't. He left out about twenty-five minutes ago, went to get his hair cut. Think he had a nine-thirty appointment at Rev's, that barber shop on 16th Street."

Regarding him with an accusatory stare, Tamia crawled

across the bed, unlocked the bedroom door, and disappeared out into the hallway. He dropped his head back and laughed, listening to Tamia's gentle footfalls as she moved throughout the apartment. He reached in his gray sweatpants and adjusted his erection, then turned and studied his own reflection in the dresser mirror.

Darren was not a pretty-boy kind of guy. He considered himself to be regular-looking, with his best feature being his dreadlocks. Chicago girls loved dreadlocks, especially when the guy the dreads were attached to was a certified gang member with a pocket full of money, adescription that Darren fit to a T. During a robbery last month, he'd managed to upgrade himself from a broke boy with less than five hundred dollars to his name to a fresh-dressed young gangster with a few pounds of Kush and over fifty thousand dollars stashed in his bedroom at his grandfather's apartment. The Ruger pistol and 30-round magazine hanging out of his sweatpants were not just for show; he was by far the most ruthless member of his gang, responsible for more than a dozen homicides this year alone.

A moment later Tamia reappeared in the doorway and Darren turned to face her. She crossed her arms over her chest, leaned a shoulder against the door-frame, and squinted at him. He grabbed his hard dick, bit down on the middle of his lower lip, and grinned at her.

"You are a complete asshole," Tamia said. "Why would you do something like that?""Why wouldn't I?"

"Well, for one," she said, her hands moving to her waist, "I'm your best friend's girlfriend.

And for two, that was borderline rape."

"Rape?" Darren scoffed at the accusation. "Let's be for real. You liked that shit. You enjoyed every minute of it."

"Just because I enjoyed it doesn't make it any less rapey….

or… creepy… you fucking creep,”

Darren pushed down the front of his sweatpants until his ten-inch phallus popped out. He looked down at it and out of the corner of his eye he saw Tamia’s mouth fall open as he began stroking it. “Kobe said he didn’t care if we fucked. He gave me the green light to ask you a few weeks ago, I just never did.”

“I’m sorry, but I absolutely cannot talk to you while you’re jacking off.” With a brief chuckle, Darren thumbed his sweats up over erection. “My bad.”“So,” Tamia asked, “Kobe actually told you to try to fuck me?”

“Yeah. Why, you don’t believe me?”

Tamia shook her head no. “Call him. I wanna hear him say it.”

“We ain’t even gotta go through that. I still got the text,” Darren said, digging in his pocket. He took out his smartphone and went to the string of text messages shared between him and Kobe.

His eyes moved to Tamia’s perfectly-built body as she walked over and snatched the phone from him. She was without a doubt one of Lawndale neighborhood’s most beautiful girls; short and sexy-faced with small breasts and a nice round ass.

“Oh, this nigga got me fucked *all* the way up,” she said, reading through the messages.“He’s been sending you all the private pictures and videos I’ve sent him, showing you my pussy.The fuck? ‘Go head and holla at her she’ll probably go. Her head game critical.’ Yeah?” She handed the phone back to Darren, grabbed a hold of his forearm, and shoved him onto the bed. “Let’s see just how *critical* this head of mine really is.”

A beaming smile spread across Darren’s dark, acne-scarred face as he watched Tamia yank down his sweatpants.

She took his steel-hard muscle in both hands and gave it a firm squeeze before she started stroking its length and kissing its head.

Just then, Darren's smartphone rang. He laughed when he saw that it was Kobe calling. Tamia saw it too; she smirked deviously and in one swift motion took his dick into her mouthand way to the rear of her throat.

"What up, G?" Darren answered.

"Bruh, tell me why I just pulled up at the barber shop and parked right behind a black Rolls- Royce. I think it's that nigga Bankroll Reese. Gotta be him. Ain't nobody else from out this way rich enough to afford a Rolls. Not unless it's Juice."

"You better be careful over there. If I was you I would've went somewhere else. We're at war with them. Don't take that shit lightly."

"Ain't nobody worried about these fuck-niggas. They ain't had no real killas ever since that lil nigga Jah moved off Trumbull last year. I got my pole on me. Fuck 'em."

Darren's toes curled up in his Jordan sneakers; this was already beginning to feel like the best head he'd ever received. His entire length was going in and out of Tamia's throat with ease and she was sucking him tightly while kneading his balls, her sweet brown eyes fixated on his.

"I feel you," Darren said.

"Is Tamia woke yet?" Kobe asked."I don't know. Hold on."

"Just shout in there and tell her to answer her phone. I'm about to call her now." Kobe hung up.

What ensued was the dirtiest act of betrayal Darren had ever seen a woman commit.

Tamia picked up her iPhone from her bedside table and then went back to sucking Darren's dick while at the same time holding a full conversation with Kobe. She was talking Kobe into pre-ordering her an iPhone 7 for her birthday when

Darren came, spewing thick white streams of semen that shot half a foot in the air before landing with an audible splat on his chest and abdomen. She muted her phone and hovered her mouth over the ropes of cum, slurping it all up.

"Mmm. That was a lot," she said, swallowing as she stood up on the bed, jumped down to the floor, and left the bedroom.

Darren got up, lit a cigarette, and trailed Tamia into the bathroom, listening as she continued her conversation as if she was truly in love with Kobe.

Chapter 1

"Most people are only good at a few things," Lee "Juice" Wilkins Sr. said as he nursed his fourth beer, "and they suck at everything else. If you want to get ahead in life, focus on the stuff you're good at and get even better."

Dawn Wilkins shot her identical twin Shawnna a look. The two of them were bustling around the kitchen table, setting up for an in-house hair appointment that was due to arrive any minute now, while their father stood a few feet away with his iPhone in one hand and his beer in the other.

He caught the look and knew what it meant. "Yeah, I know I'm just another drug-dealin' ass Vice Lord, but that's only because when I was a shorty it's what everybody around me was. It's all I ever knew. But you two, on the other hand, have the chance of a lifetime, the chance I never had. Y'all went to Paul Mitchell, the best hair school in the world, and became licensed hair stylists."

"Master cosmetologists," Shawnna interjected.

"Same difference," Juice said. "Point is, you've found something you're good at. Practice as much as possible and become even better at it. Utilize Malcolm Gladwell's 10,000-hour rule. That way you'll eventually be just as highly-regarded in your profession as Steve Jobs and Michael Jordan are in theirs. If you want to make a nice living, get really good at one thing and you'll be unstoppable."

Shawnna sighed loudly and offered Juice the same look Dawn had given her less than a minute prior. It was always easy to tell when he had some alcohol coursing through his veins. Whenever he started giving wise advice and couldn't seem to put an end to it, he was more than likely on the brink of intoxication. Under normal circumstances she would have called him outon it, but compassion held her back from doing it now. He'd been drinking a lot during the last few weeks and his reason for doing so was understandable. Twenty days ago they'd buried his only son, seventeen-year-old Lee Wilkins Jr. The following morning he'd been served divorce papers from his wife, who he had caught in bed with Carol – her so-called "best friend" – on the night of his son's murder.

Juice had hardly left the house since Junior's funeral. He was in an ocean-deep state of grief, practically drowning in it, which was why Shawnna was standing here in his small kitchen instead of being at her wealthy boyfriend's Burr Ridge mansion where she belonged.

Despite the big man's palpable grief, his inclination to hustle had not changed one bit. While lying in bed upstairs four nights ago, Shawnna had overheard Juice and her cousin talking abouta major drug deal just outside her bedroom door. She'd tip-toed across the room to the door and listened.

"Reese hit my line a few hours ago," her cousin Kev had said. "Said he wanna grab twenty this go around, if you can get 'em for the price you mentioned the other night."

"I told him twenty-seven.""That's what he said."

"Damn, did he already run through the ten?"

"Nah. Still working on that. He got some nigga in Cleveland trying to cop some weight and two other niggas in Detroit. Think he's taxing them thirty-six racks for every block. It's Grindo'speople."

Juice had paused for a brief moment. "A'ight, tell him to come on with the bread. I really wasn't planning on making no more moves this summer, but I can't turn down the lil homie. I need the extra cash anyway. Gotta drop damn near seventy thousand on the hair salon for the twins."

"Be strong, Unc. I see the pain on your face. As soon as we find out who killed Junior it's gon' be another murder scene."

Back in her bed, Shawnna had ruminated over everything

she'd heard. The hair salon news excited her; the revelation that her dad had twenty kilos shocked her. And true to his word, Juice had twenty kilograms of cocaine delivered to Reese by noontime the next day; Shawnna was there when Kev dropped them off.

Now that Shawnna knew just how powerful her father was when it came to Chicago's drug trade, she wondered where he was keeping all the money and how much he actually had. Reese had once called her dad Mr. 1008 Grams. She now understood why.

Juice was starting to look like money. He had on a heavy-looking gold Cuban link necklace and a gold Rolex watch. He hadn't showered since yesterday morning, but his black t-shirt and black sweatpants were still relatively clean and they were expensive. His black sneakers were Christian Louboutin, like the five inch heels Dawn and Shawnna were wearing, and they'd cost him fifteen hundred dollars.

His outfit was as dark as his mood, but Shawnna had a remedy for her father's grief.

If there was one person in all of Chicago who could brighten Juice's spirits, it was the woman who was due to arrive here at his west side home at precisely 10:00 A.M.

Shawnna glanced at the microwave to see the time. It was five minutes to ten.

Chapter 2

Juice's heart abandoned its post and lowered itself to snuggle up next to his stomach when Lakita "Bubbles" Thomas came sauntering through the back door and into the kitchen, preceded by Myesha, the girl next in line to get her hair done by the Wilkins twins.

Brown-complected, pretty-faced, and improbably big-bottomed, Bubbles was – like Myesha

– one of Redbone's Gentleman's Club's most sought after dancers. Her eye-popping, jaw- dropping curves had gotten her into and on the covers of dozens of urban "booty" magazines. After seeing her in a Lil Wayne music video when he was in prison four years ago, Juice had found her photos in *Straight Stuntin* and *Black Lingerie* magazines and glued them to the wall in his cell. He'd watched her love life unfold on TV shows like *TMZ* and *Dish Nation*, where her high profile romances with several rap stars and professional athletes had been presented to the world. He told the guys in Stateville that once he was released and got a few thousand dollars in his pocket, he was going to the strip club where Bubbles worked and meet her. He'd stuck to his word and it was love at first lap dance.

"Hey, Juice." Bubbles walked over and gave him a quick hug, then turned to greet the twins.

Juice enjoyed the hug – the scent of her fragrance, the feel of her body against his – but it was the sight of her backside as she turned away from him that really got him going. Her gray denim shorts seemed to have been painted on. Juice was a sucker for a big butt and a smile, the former of which Bubbles had an abundance.

The sudden realization that he had neglected to shower on this scaring-hot summer day hit Juice like a crowbar to the skull. He excused himself and went to the master bedroom, his mind swarming with images of Bubbles, many of them X-rated.

His wife had moved out of the house three weeks ago. Her absence was most apparent in the bedroom, where they had slept together for more than a thousand nights. With all of her things gone the bedroom looked a lot less cluttered and a hell of a lot more habitable.

He'd already laid out an outfit on the bed: a black Balmain shirt, an undershirt and jeans by the same high-end designer, a two-tone black Louis Vuitton belt, and a pair of black Air Force Ones. Everything was brand-new, a clear sign that his financial situation was getting better bythe day.

Thanks to his Mexican cocaine plug, Juice now had well over a half million dollars in cash, all hidden away in various locations just in case his home was ever raided by police.

He crossed the hallway to the bathroom and undressed, still thinking about Bubbles and hoping she wouldn't be gone when he returned to the kitchen. Needless to say, he took what was undoubtedly the fastest shower he'd ever taken and he cut his head twice in his haste to shave it.

He was dressed and spraying a bit of cologne across the chest of his shirt when his cellphone vibrated and his nephew Kevin's picture flashed on its screen. "Yo?" he answered.

"What it is, Uncle?"

"Not shit, Nephew. Just hopped out the shower, got shaved up real nice. Why, what y'all on?"

"You gotta see for yourself. Meet us over here at Rev's Barber Shop on 16th. We got asurprise for you."

"No, no, no. Bullshit, nigga. I wouldn't leave if this house was on fire right now." Juice wassmiling for the first time since his son's murder almost a month earlier.

"Juice, you gotta get outta that house. I understand- "

"No you don't. I got the prettiest, most big-bootied bad

bitch in the city sitting downstairs inmy kitchen. Ain't no way I'm leaving."

"Who you talking about? Bubbles?"

"And you know it. Myesha came to get her hair done, and Bubbles came with her. I got two fifths of Remy and a whole lot of pills – OxyContins, Xanax, Percocets, you name it I got it.Only got about a half ounce of loud left, but it'll do."

"Okay... I guess we'll just have to bring the surprise to you," Kev said and ended the call abruptly.

Juice took out all the things he had in the pockets of his worn sweats – a black leather wallet,a folded stack of hundred-dollar bills, a set of keys, and a Ziploc bag containing numerous sandwich bags of pills and weed – and stuffed it all into the pockets of his exorbitantly priced designer jeans. He gave himself a final once-over, put his .40-caliber Glock pistol on his hip, and then left the bathroom taking the stairs two at a time in his race to rejoin his daughters and their two stripper friends in the kitchen.

Chapter 3

Roughly forty percent of the boys and men in North Lawndale relied on Rev's Barber Shop for their hair cuts. Situated directly across the street from Redbone's – the west side's premiere strip club – and right next door to an old game room that was now being renovated and reshaped into a hair salon, Rev's was a hot spot for local drug dealers and gang members, as well as the regular nine-to-fivers who valued freedom and family over reputation and riches.

Kobe's reason for choosing such an early time slot for his hair cut was simple: the barber shop was smack-dab in the middle of a predominantly Vice Lord neighborhood and the gang Kobe was a member of – the Black Gangsters, also known as the New Breeds – was at war with the Vice Lords in this area. It was best to get in and get out early, before the pill-popping gunslingers woke up and hit the streets.

Of the nine leather barber chairs in the shop, just two of them were occupied. Kobe sat inone and, just as he'd suspected, Bankroll Reese was in the other chair getting his hair cut by Rev while Rev's brother Bernard cut Kobe's. The two huge men who served as Reese's bodyguards –Chubb and Suwu – were standing outside next to the Rolls-Royce, chatting it up with Reese's uncle Kevin.

There were a few things Kobe and Reese had in common. One, they were both remarkably handsome young men from here on the west side. Two, they were both in love with the same woman. After ending it with Kobe, Shawnna Wilkins had moved on to Reese.

The comparisons ended there. Kobe's snow-white 1980's-model Chevy Caprice on matching 28-inch rims was nice-looking and worth twenty grand, but it paled in comparison to the triple-black Rolls-Royce Phantom Drophead Coupe that was parked in front of Kobe's ride. The fortune Reese had inherited from his father was estimated to be somewhere in the neighborhood of $60 million, a net worth that made the lousy $3,100 Kobe had in his pocketlook like pennies.

"I'm surprised to see you in here," Bernard said. "With all the beef niggas got with y'allover there on 13th, I figured we wouldn't be seeing you for a while."

"You know I don't get involved in all that. If it ain't about a check I ain't got time for it. Been coming through here since Rev first opened this joint. Gotta support the gang." Kobe put on a triumphant smile. He was exploiting the fact that Rev was also a Black Gangster, though Rev, nearing forty, had retired from the street life years ago.

Rev's real name was Cory Tuff. An appreciative grin blossomed on his face when he heard Kobe's supportive words. He was not exactly ugly, but he looked peculiar, as if he'd been conjured in a cauldron by a coven of wicked witches. He was snaggle-toothed and the stench of cognac seemed to be drifting out of his pores. Nevertheless, Rev was a successful business owner and a respected OG, dressed clean and casual in a t-shirt and jeans.

"I'll give you that," Rev said, nodding his head affirmatively. "I'll definitely give you that.

You've been in here every other Friday since the day I first opened. That's some real shit, G."

"Gotta stay fresh for the hoes." Kobe gave Reese a look. "A fresh fade keep me with a bad bitch."

Reese chuckled once, but he didn't bite. He continued scrolling down an Instagram page on his iPhone. Flawless white diamonds, some as big and round as marbles, glistened in the five necklaces hanging around his neck and the two rings on his pinkie fingers. His Rolex watch was also full of white diamonds. If not for his armed bodyguards standing out front, constantly looking in through the windows to check on him, Kobe would have pulled his gun and demandedthat Reese hand over the jewelry.

"What's up, Bankroll?" Kobe was far too hungry for riches to let this chance encounter with the multimillionaire pass by. "What I gotta do to get in on some of that big money? That Cup Gang money. Plug me in."

Without so much as a glance in Kobe's direction, Reese said, "I got fifty bands for you… if you can tell me where to find Darren and Big Jay."

Kobe's eyes lit up. "Fifty thousand dollars? You serious?"

"Don't waste my time. Either you know where to find 'em or you don't know where to find 'em."

Brooding over the offer, Kobe nodded slowly. Big Jay was yet another Black Gangster, released just days ago from Cook County Jail after the sole witness in the double homicide for which he'd been in custody for changed her story and fled to Atlanta. Big Jay had shown up at Tamia's apartment a couple of times since his release from jail. He and Darren were close, and they looked a lot alike – long dreadlocks, dark complexions, icy demeanors. The two of them were considered the most ruthless members of the gang. Kobe liked having them around, but only for protection. In other words, he could do without them.

"I can probably set it up," he said, his head frozen in place as Bernard gave him a line-up. "Either you can or you can't. I don't need no fuckin' probably."

"I can do it. Give me a day or two. I'll make sure they're together. That way it'll be easier, you know? Let me get your number so I can hit your line when I get this shit lined up."

"Just give your number to Suwu. He'll call you from a number you can contact." Finally, Reese turned to look at Kobe. "I already know that it was Big Jay and Darren who whacked my nigga Lil Dave. What I don't know is who killed Junior last month.

"It was Darren," Kobe said. "He killed Junior with the same AK-47 they used to kill Head and Lil Dave."

Bankroll Reese nodded his head thoughtfully. Then he went back to perusing Instagram on his smartphone, looking like a Chicagoan who'd swapped wardrobes with Floyd "Money"Mayweather Jr.

A huge sense of relief washed over Kobe, setting off a grin that grew and grew and grew as he realized that Reese had no idea it was Kobe's car that had pulled up alongside Junior's Cadillac that fateful night one month ago. Darren had opened fire from the back seat. In stunned silence, Kobe had watched as round after devastating round ripped through the Cadillac's passenger's side, effectively finishing the youthful lives of Lee Wilkins Jr. and his girlfriend Christina. Momentarily, Kobe had teared up, his heart heavy with emotion at having witnessed the murder of his former brother-in-law. Then, he'd spun the steering wheel to his right and careened down Trumbull Avenue, reminding himself that Junior's murder was in retaliation for the half a dozen Black Gangsters who'd been shot to death that month, guys he'd spent nearly every day of his life around. In the weeks since Junior's murder Kobe had done his best to avoid traveling through this particular stretch of North Lawndale for fear that he might meet the same fate. Now, knowing that Reese didn't know about his involvement in the shooting, Kobe felt at ease.

He peeled a twenty and a ten out of his knot of cash, handed the thirty dollars to Bernard,and left out the front door of Rev's, moving less cautiously than he head when he arrived thirty minutes earlier.

There was a four-door Bentley sitting in front of the Phantom. It too was blacked out, very presidential-looking, and

Suwu's massive body was reclined in the passenger's seat. He was lighting a blunt while Kev, behind the wheel, rolled a second one.

Chubb, the bigger of the two top-heavy bodyguards, was standing at Suwu's door with a half-eaten double cheeseburger in one hand and a cup with a lid and a straw in the other.

Suwu looked at Kobe. "You smoke?"

"What kinda question is that? Do you breathe, nigga?" Kobe took three steps back as a pregnant woman and a teenage boy passed him on the sidewalk. Once he verified that the teen wasn't a threat, he stepped forward to his previous spot at the Bentley's passenger door. Suwu handed him the blunt and he took a deep pull on it.

"Scary-ass lil nigga." Suwu laughed.

"Too scary," Kev said. "The hell you just back up like that for?"

"You never know these days," Kobe said. "I can't even count all the niggas I done lost this year. Gotta watch everybody." He drew in another lungful of weed smoke and passed the bluntin to Kev. "Suwu, I gotta give you my number. Reese just told me to give it to you."

Suwu produced a smartphone. "Give it to me."

Kobe gave it to him. "That's my cell number. I always got it on me. Man, try to make sure he hit me up. He got some bread for me and I need it. Bad. For real."

"If he got something for you, you'll get it," Kev assured, leaning back in his seat and blowing smoke up at the rear-view mirror. "Get in the back if you wanna smoke. We can hit a few corners."

Kobe had done a lot of hanging out with Kev when he and Shawnna were together, so hewas not at all hesitant to get in the back seat. Plus, he'd never been in a Bentley before. As soon as he got in Kev pulled off.

Chapter 4

"Bubbles, let me get a minute with you… in the living room." Juice was grabbing a bottle of Remy out of the freezer and a couple of White Owl cigars from a box on top of the refrigerator. In his periphery, he saw the twins roll their eyes in unison and heard the crisp sucking of their teeth. Impervious to the haters, he strode out of the kitchen and into the living room, aplomb and overflowing with confidence. Alcohol – both the idea and the consumption of it – had a way of filling Juice with an abundance of confidence.

He flopped down on the rich brown leather L-shaped sectional sofa and poured himself a cup of Remy. He was just setting the bottle down on the carpeted floor between his sneakers when Bubbles joined him. She put a hand on his knee as she eased down onto the sofa. He turned to her, a smile growing. Hers was a wider smile, a heart-melting smile situated beneath sparkling brown eyes. Combine her beautiful face with her meaty ass and thighs, wide hips, and small waist, and it was easy to understand why, like most guys who met her, Juice could not keep his eyes off of her. She'd played a starring role in many of his fantasies and today he was hoping to bring those fantasies to reality.

"Look at you," she said, studying his attire.

"Look at you," he echoed. "Seems like you get thicker and thicker every time I see you." "Oh, please. If anything I'm getting skinnier. I've lost almost fifteen pounds this summer.

Me and Myesha are in the gym four or five days a week and I wear my waist-trainer four hours a day now."

Juice shook his head disapprovingly, drank from his cup, and said, "I can't believe you actually think waist-trainers work. That's a scam, in my opinion."

"And you know what they say about opinions."

"To each his own." Splitting open a cigar, he shrugged. "On another note, what's going on with you? Relationship-wise, I mean. You with somebody? Last time I asked for your number you didn't give it to me."

"Yeah, because you were married," Bubbles said, speaking slowly and enunciating each word like a daycare worker laying down the ground rules to a room full of bad-ass ghetto children. "I'm sorry, but I don't date married men. I had a traumatic experience dealing with a married man last year and I promised myself that I would never go through that again. But I heard about what happened with you and your wife, the whole divorce thing, so I guess that makes you fair game."

"Who told you about that?"

"Chandra's been telling everybody about it. She said you and her were messing around, but neither of you knew that her mom and your wife were messing around until you walked in on them. From what I recall her saying it was that night I last saw you in Redbone's, the night your son and his girl got… you know." Her hand went to his knee again. She patted it twice, shaking her head. "I'm so sorry. I can't even begin to imagine the pain you must be going through. My daughter is everything to me. I'd lose my mind if I lost her."

Juice took a deep breath and a large gulp of Remy. He fished his iPhone and the Ziploc bag of drugs out of his pocket, placed them on the glass-topped coffee table, and dropped a few buds of the Kush into the now empty cigar wrapper.

"Have y'all found out who shot him?" Bubbles asked.

Juice swallowed some more Remy. With his teeth just shy of a clench, he said, "No. No, we haven't. But we will… and when we do it's gon' be ugly." He changed the subject. "You drink? Want me to get you a cup?"

"Boy are you crazy? It's not even noon yet.""Is that some

kind of law?"

She rolled her eyes. "Maybe later. We can smoke, though."

"So there will be a later? For us? Tonight?" He laughed at himself. "I sound way too thirsty, don't I?"

"Yes. Very."

"Can you blame me? I mean, shit, you're my mother-fuckin' *crush*. I can't name one woman I like more than I like you. That's the honest-to-God truth."

"Spitting game went out of style ten years ago." With a sexy wise-ass grin, she picked up a cigar and removed its plastic wrapper. "To be honest, I've had my eye on you for a while. You're a lot wiser than the guys I'm used to dating. Older, too."

"I ain't that damn old."

"Calm down. It's actually a good thing. I'm starting to think that it might be better to date guys who are older than me. The life expectancy for guys my age is horrible. The last three niggas who've tried to get with me are dead, all because they wanted to gangbang. We never even had the chance to fuck."

"See, that's the problem. There's a difference between a gang member and gangbanger. Gang members get money to take care of our families and to keep the mob eating. All gangbangers do is hunt each other down. I just want the money; they can keep all that other shit. Beef is for broke niggas. My only goal now is to leave my daughters with enough money to live comfortably and enough wisdom to become even wealthier."

"I know that's right, Grandpa." Bubbles showed her sexy wise-ass grin again. Her phone rang as she was rolling the blunt. She glanced at the number and ignored the call.

Juice didn't ask.

Instead, he struck a flame from his plastic Bic lighter and

waved it along the length of his blunt, drying it. His mind wandered aimlessly. He thought of his son's killer's identity and pondered whether or not the fifty-thousand-dollar bounty he'd put on the shooter's head would do any good. He summoned a recently created fantasy of Bubbles sitting naked on his face in the middle of his bed, then tried to vanquish the erotic image from his mind's eye when it caused his dick to swell like an inflating bicycle tire.

"Is that your dick?"

The sound of her voice snapped Juice out of his reverie. He looked at her and saw that she was staring intently at the crotch of his jeans.

"Ooh and it's throbbing," she said, giggling sweetly. She boldly reached over and caressed his growing bulge. Her eyes twinkled. "Oh, my God, it's *huge*! How big *is* it? Have you ever *measured* this thing?"

"Now who's sounding thirsty?" Juice chuckled, his alcohol-induced confidence burgeoning.

Of course he'd measured himself before. What man hadn't? The very first time he had put a ruler to his Johnson was in middle school, when he was about thirteen or fourteen years old and just starting to become sexually active. The first measurement had been a quarter shy of nine inches and by the time he was sixteen his dick had grown to a staggering twelve inches when fully erect, which was the same length as his present-day erections at the youthful age of thirty- four.

"I need that in my life," Bubbles said, unable to take her eyes off his bulge as she pulled the invasive hand back and sighed out loud. "Your wife must really have some serious mental issues. There is no way I would've divorced a dick that big. Till death do us part, nigga. Bullshit ain't nothin'. But then again, her ass didn't want a man to begin with."

Juice lit the blunt and puffed a couple of times. The truth in what Bubbles had just said was sobering enough to make him take another drink. He had walked in and caught his wife getting fucked by her coworker friend Carol, who'd been wearing a strap-on dildo. It was an indelible memory; he wished he could forget it, but that was an impossibility.

"So," Bubbles asked as he passed her the blunt, "is it over? Is the divorce final? Because I know how that stuff can be dragged out for months or sometimes years."

"Nah, it's over. We're officially divorced. The judge gave me ninety days to move out of here and put the house on the market. We'll split the money and go on about our business."

"Have you found a place?"

"Looked at a few. Ain't made no decisions. I might just give somebody the money to buy it, then have them sign it over to me. Or something like that. Gotta talk to my lawyer about it."

"Is the house the only thing you lost?"

Juice nodded. "This and that Cadillac truck I bought her."

"Fuck that Cadillac truck. That Jaguar truck you pulled up to the club in that night is still the hardest truck in the city. Bitches ain't stopped talking about that yet."

The silver Jaguar F-Pace SUV was now hidden away in the garage at his mother's house in Bellwood, Illinois. He'd only driven it twice – once on the night of Junior's murder, and a second time on the day of Junior's funeral. Since then he'd been driving Shawnna and Dawn's red Dodge Chargers whenever he needed to go out, which was not often.

"I'm heading out to my mama's to get it today," he said, though he had planned on travelingto get it tomorrow evening.

"Really?" Bubbles said. "You should let me drive it.""You should let me fuck."

"You're gonna have to do a lot more than smoke some weed with me and let me drive your truck to get some of this pussy. I'm not into one-night stands. A lot of guys think that, just because I'm a stripper – "

"Don't compare me to them."

"I'm not… I'm just saying." "I'm not like everybody else."

"That's what they all say." She gazed thoughtfully at the blunt pinched between her thumb and forefinger, smoke billowing from her nostrils. "You know, I honestly haven't had sex in a long time. It's literally been almost fourteen months."

"I don't believe that," Juice said.

"I swear on my life, I haven't had a dick in me – a real one, I mean – since last July.""Why must July to me?" Juice joked.

Bubbles laughed once. "You know what?" She raised a middle finger. She had a thin diamond bracelet on her wrist and a few diamond rings on her fingers, including the finger she was holding up. Her hoop earrings and necklace were also shimmering with diamonds. The earrings – like her shirt, belt, shoes and purse – was Chanel.

Leaning toward her, Juice poised his lips for a kiss and managed to land one on her pinkie knuckle as Bubbles lowered her hand. She didn't react to the show of affection. She passed the blunt back to him. He put an elbow on the armrest. Blunt in one hand, cup in the other, he sat back, smoking and drinking and regarding Bubbles the way Jay Z must have regarded QueenBey the first time she'd sat next to him.

"It's gonna take the twins about two or three hours to get Myesha's hair done," Bubbles said, checking her smartphone. "Soon's we finish this blunt I'm taking my ass home to watch *Narcos* on Netflix. I'll come back and pick her up."

"*Narcos*!" Juice's red eyes went wide and he lifted himself from the sofa. "That's my favorite show. Pablo Escobar was that nigga. I got it paused on my TV right now. Come on."

He was full of shit. Over the past couple of weeks he had

watched two episodes of *Flash*, four episodes of *Gotham*, twelve minutes and twenty-two seconds of the *Cartel Land* documentary, and the movie *Brotherly Love* on Netflix, but not once had he watched *Narcos*. He only knew what it was about from seeing posts about it on Facebook.

If Bubbles saw through the lie she didn't show it. She helped him gather his things and then shadowed him to the stairwell that led up to his bedroom.

"We'll be upstairs watching *Narcos*, y'all," she shouted to the girls as they stared up the wooden staircase.

"Bullshit," Myesha shouted back.

"Girl," Dawn yelled, "don't be up there giving my daddy no damn lap dances. This is the Wilkins household, not Redbone's."

Nearing the top of the stairs, Juice looked back at Bubbles. Both of them were laughing. She had the dark green Remy Martin bottle in her right hand. The twinkle had returned to her eyes. Her long, thick legs extended from her tiny denim jeans in the most amazing way.

He halted at his bedroom door and stepped aside, motioning for her to go in ahead of him. "Ladies first," he said.

"Mmm hmm," she replied skeptically, giving him the side eye.

She entered the bedroom, and Juice fell in step behind her, gawking at the deliciously round mounds of flesh stuffed in her shorts. He shut the door, closed the distance between them, and slapped a hand onto her rear left pocket, biting the tip of his tongue like he always did when he was in the mood.

Bubbles turned to face him so that they were nose to nose and for a moment they silently gazed into each other's eyes. His hand remained on her ass, squeezing and pulling, slapping and pushing.

"The TV isn't even on," she said, with a trace of amusement in her gentle voice."I noticed that, too. I don't know what happened."

"Sure you don't."

"I'm dead-ass serious. You might be right about me getting old. I'm getting forgetful.

Alzheimer's must be kicking in.""Forget my ass."

"That's impossible." He gave it another smack. "I'll forget my own name before I forgetanything about you."

His dick was hard again; it made a tent in the crotch of his jeans and poked at Bubbles' thigh. She looked down at it and exhaled loudly.

"You are really trying me," she said, licking her top lip.

Then, they heard a loud crash from somewhere downstairs and all hell broke loose.

Chapter 5

"Bitch," Darren shouted as he stormed into the kitchen after having kicked open the back door of Juice's two-story redbrick home, "get on the floor!"

He waved the pistol in front of him, scowling through the eye-holes of his ski-mask. RoRo- G came in behind him, also masked and toting a nine-millimeter Glock.

Darren immediately recognized all three of the girls: they were Shawnna and Dawn, the Wilkins twins, and Myesha, the baddest stripper Darren had ever laid eyes on. He'd seen Myesha in action when she used to dance at The Factory. She was the truth.

The three girls screamed, startled by the masked gunmen.

Grabbing a handful of Shawnna's hair (or Dawn's; with the two being identical twins, he couldn't tell the difference), he put the barrel of his gun to the side of her head.

Just thirteen years old, RoRo-G was with the shit. He shoved the other twin to the floor, then turned and slapped Myesha with his gun, knocking her down next to the twin.

"What's your name?" Darren hissed in his captive's ear. "My daddy is going to fucking kill you," she said. "Don't make me shoot you."

"Am I supposed to be scared?""You should be."

Lying face-down on the tiled kitchen floor, the other twin said, "Shawnna, just do what he says so he can leave."

"Yeah, Shawnna," Darren said. "Take me to your daddy's safe – or his shoe boxes. Wherever he hides all that money. That's all I'm here for. Now you can either give me that shitor die like your brother did. It's all on you."

He felt her body go rigid against his. Her pretty face became a mask of fiery anger. Darren smiled briefly. Adrenaline rocketed through his veins like NASCAR drivers.

As RoRo-G unpocketed a roll of duct tape and kneeled down near Dawn and Myesha's legs, Darren shoved Shawnna forward. She was obviously reluctant to walk, but she walked; past the kitchen table and into a short hallway. Straight ahead was a living room, but it was the start of a staircase they were approaching to their right that held Darren's attention.

He turned to face the stairwell as they moved toward it, keeping Shawnna directly in front of him; if anyone was waiting on the stairs to ambush him, Shawnna would get hit first.

His quick thinking paid off.

Juice was standing on the fifth stair with a gun aimed right at him.

"Nigga, you got two seconds," Darren snapped, his expression beneath the mask matching the fury of Shawnna's.

It didn't take two seconds. Juice extended his arm and released his hold on the pistol.

Darren contemplated shooting Juice dead right then and there. After all, Juice was the leaderof the gang that had been gunning down members of Darren's gang. B-Man and Cash Boy, Darren's childhood friends, had lost their lives last month in shootings that were rumored to havebeen ordered by Juice.

Despite his beef with Juice and the Traveler Vice Lords, Darren didn't take aim at Juice and pull the trigger. He was here for the drug money. Like most of the guys in the area, Darren knew that the majority of crack and coke being sold on the west side streets came from Juice. Darren had been plotting the robbery for weeks, but it was not until this morning, when he had Tamia pinned against her shower wall with his dick deep inside her, that he'd decided to carry out his robbery plan.

He wanted to run away with Tamia and he wanted to have a lot of money when he did it.

Juice raised his hands over his head. "Let her go," he

pleaded. "She ain't got nothing to do with this."

"Nah, nigga. Shit don't work like that. Lead me to the money before I fuck around and shootthis bitch."

"It's up here. Just… chill out." Juice turned around slowly, but he went up the stairs rather hastily.

Darren was unbothered by Juice's swiftness. He scooped up the pistol Juice had dropped andjammed it into Shawnna's lower back, forcing her to climb the stairs just as quickly and eliciting from her a muffled cry of pain.

In the kitchen, RoRo-G was still busy taping Dawn and Myesha's wrists and ankles together; Darren could hear the tape being ripped from the roll.

"Hurry up and get them taped up, G!" Darren said as Juice led the way into a sparselyfurnished bedroom.

"On my way in one minute, big G!" RoRo-G shouted back.

Darren noticed that there was a blunt roach burning in an ashtray beside a chilled bottle of Remy on a cherry-wood bedside table. A second, unburned blunt lay next to the ashtray along with a red plastic cup and a bag of pills. A silver-framed photograph of Juice and his three children – Junior and the twins – acted as a centerpiece on the table. Knowing that it was him who'd murdered Junior rattled Darren's nerves a little, but not much. He'd done worse.

"It's all right here in the closet," Juice said, standing with his back to the closet door and his hands in the air, eyeing Darren cautiously.

"Well?" Darren asked, slipping Juice's pistol into the belly pocket of his gray hoodie, "Whatthe fuck are you waiting for? Open up the goddamn closet. I ain't got all day."

"Listen, I'll give you every dollar I got. All I ask is that you not hurt my daugh –"

"All I ask is that you *shut the fuck up and gimme the mon-*

ey! Keep on talking and see if I don't kill you *and* this bitch."

"Okay, man. Okay." Juice turned around and pulled open the closet door. He squatted down on his haunches and began spinning the combination wheel on a gray steel safe that stood about two and a half feet off of the floor.

Darren's heart skipped a beat (or at least that's how it felt) and he stopped breathing forwhat must have been five or six seconds as Juice pulled open the safe door and moved aside.

Jackpot!

The safe was crammed full of cash, thick piles rubber-banded together and stacked to the safe's ceiling. Darren felt like doing Bobby Shmurda's "Shmoney Dance," he was so elated. Then, he considered doing Plies's "Ran Off On the Plug Twice" dance. Finally, he settled on doing no dances, at least until he was out of there with the money.

He gave Shawnna a hard push that sent her sprawling onto the bed. "If you do as I say you'lllive," he threatened. "If you don't, on the guys I'm killing everybody in this house. Now… take the pillowcases off those pillows and put all that money in 'em. Both of y'all. And hurry up."

Holding Juice and his gorgeous daughter at gunpoint, Darren watched as they started filling the pillowcases. He was already spending the money in his head. He would start by renting himself a cheap apartment somewhere in the suburbs and using it as a place to stash his money and lay low. His next purchase would be an SUV of some kind. Then, maybe he would get a second apartment near the first one and get Tamia to move into it with him. That was the best- case scenario. If she didn't want to move in with him, he was fine with that too. He'd get anotherbad bitch. If all else failed, there was always *Backpage* to fall back on.

It took three pillow cases to hold all the bills. Juice and Shawnna were done filling them by the time RoRo-G walked in.

"Had to drag them hoes to the living room," RoRo-G said, sounding halfway out of breath. "Didn't wanna leave 'em in the kitchen with the door broke open like it is. Somebody mightwalk in."

"Smart." Darren picked up the cash-filled pillowcases. "I got the bread. Search around up here and see if you can find anything else, then come down and help me get these two taped upso we can go."

Feeling confident that he had successfully pulled off the robbery he'd been planning for more than a month, Darren ushered Juice and Shawnna back down the stairs at gunpoint. There was a framed painting of Jesus on the cross mounted on the stairwell wall that he hadn't noticed when they came up the stairs. Passing the crucifixion, he silently mouthed "God forgive me,"and made a mental note to stop by his grandmother's church in the coming days with a gratuitousdonation.

He took a handful of Shawnna's shirt in the fist he held the pillowcases in and he held the gun to the back of her head with his other hand as he made it into the living room.

Dawn and Myesha were bound in similar fashion, with tape covering their mouths and holding their wrists and ankles together. The only thing different about the way the two of them were restrained was the extra layers of tape around Myesha's ankles and that her jeans and underwear were pulled down to her knees. They were stretched out in front of the sofa, so Darren made Juice and Shawnna lie down on their stomachs behind the sofa with their hands behindtheir heads.

"To tell you the truth," Darren said, "I was gon' kill you, Juice. I really was. Y'all been fucking us up for so long. And I know it's gotta be you who keeps buying the guns for them to do that shit. Either you or Bankroll Reese and in my eyes y'all are one and the same. I actually thought it was you in that red 'Lac I shot up. I knew it was your car and that big-ass nigga Junior looked just like you."

Juice's hands slowly became fists on the back of his head.

"Ha!" Darren laughed. "You got a lil' frog in you, nigga? Jump your tough ass up. I toldyou, I already wanna kill you. Gimme a reason. *Please* gimme a reason. I'ma slaughter every single one of you bitches. I'd stay on that floor if I were you. I really would. Doing anything else will get me all upset, and trust me, that's not what you want. Niggas die when I get upset."

Darren would have kept up the verbal abuse, but a sudden knock on the front door silenced him. His eyes darted from the door to Juice and back to the door as someone started repeatedly ringing the doorbell.

Upstairs, RoRo-G yelled, "Oh, shit! Darren!"

The scream was followed by what sounded like a shotgun blast.

Startled by the sudden turn of events, Darren turned and fled out the back door he'd kickedin minutes earlier.

Chapter 6

There was a small, cramped closet just inside of the front door of the Wilkins home, and in the closet, leaned against the side wall, was an AR-15 assault rifle with red laser sighting and a 120-round drum magazine. Thinking of only the fact that his son's killer was escaping, Juice ran to the closet, grabbed the assault rifle, and rushed to the back door. He made it onto the back porch just in time to see the masked gunman starting the engine of a rusty white Nissan sedan that had to be at least fifteen years old. It was parked in the alley, facing east.

Without any hesitation, Juice lifted the assault rifle and pulled the trigger five times in rapid succession as the Nissan's rear tires churned up a cloud of dirt, rocks, and debris and sent it soaring away. Each pull of the trigger launched a three-round burst of ammunition that peppered the Nissan with holes, essentially turning its passenger's side into mesh. The gunfire was deafening, but Juice hardly noticed it. Smoking-hot gun shells rained down onto the wooden porch.

Juice briefly considered chasing after the escaping vehicle on foot, but then he remembered that his daughters were still inside with the second gunman and his paternal instincts took over.

When he returned to the living room, all four of the girls were boo-hooing on each other's shoulders, and the Remington 870 Brushmaster 12-gauge shotgun Juice kept in the hallway closet upstairs was on the sofa with the Chanel bag Bubbles had had on her arm when he last saw her. The twins were hugging. Bubbles and Myesha were locked in a consoling embrace. Kev must have been the doorbell-ringer, because he was just coming down from upstairs with Suwu, who was his wife Tara's brother and also one of Bankroll Reese's bodyguards. Both of them had pistols in hand.

"Man," Kev said, shaking his yellowish-brown-skinned head and taking off his Bulls fitted cap, "I don't know who the fuck that lil nigga is up there in that hallway, but he is definitely overwith. Homie got his whole top knocked off."

"I can't believe I killed someone," Bubbles said, still sobbing and sniffling as she detached herself from Myesha. "I was going to just try scaring him with it. But he had a gun. He had a *gun*."

"I know." Juice pulled her in for a one-armed hug. "It'll be okay. A'ight? Don't get yourself all worked up and stressed out over it. You did what you had to do." He rubbed a hand up and down her back, planted a kiss on her forehead, and shook his head in disbelief.

Kev moved close to Juice and put his mouth an inch from Juice's left ear. "We got thatnigga Kobe with us. You know they say it was his car that fired the shots at Junior."

Through clenched teeth, Juice asked, "Where he at?"

"On the front porch. Told him to stay outside out of respect for Reese and Shawnna." "Good." Juice handed the AR-15 to Kev. "Here, take this and get outta here. And put that
fuck-nigga in the trunk."

Chapter 7

"Oh, *hell* no! Really, Darren?! What the fuck happened to my car?"

"What the fuck you think happened?" Darren's tone of voice was full of sarcasm. He breezed past Tamia with the pillowcases swinging at his side, leaving her standing at the door with her hands on her hips, staring outside at her bullet-riddled vehicle.

"You said you and RoRo was going to the store up the street. How in the hell did this end uphappening?"

"Close that door."

"Tell me what's going on," Tamia said, slamming the door shut. "Do you know how long I had to save up to get that car? Two whole years. And since I don't have insurance, that's twenty- eight hundred dollars down the fucking drain. That's going to be impossible to replace."

Darren started disconnecting his Xbox One from Tamia's living room TV. His heart was pounding in his chest. He looked at Tamia and smiled.

"This is so not funny, D. I am oh-so motherfucking serious."

"I know you're serious. You don't think you can patch a hole up? Or find somebody to do it?"

Tamia crossed her arms and her eyes became stringent slits.

"I'm just playing with you." Darren chuckled, dropped the disconnected cords to the carpeted floor, and then took a rubber-banded bundle of fifties from one of the pillowcases. "Youlook so sexy when you're mad. Been wanting to tell you that for a while now."

Her interest piqued, Tamia walked around the sofa, moving closer to Darren as he snapped the rubber band and thumbed through the bills. She got a glimpse of what was inside one of the pillowcases at Darren's feet; she put her hands over her mouth and gasped.

"I'll give you twenty-eight hundred for the car," Darren said, "plus another three thousand togo shopping with. All you gotta do is agree to leave with me right now and stay with me for the weekend."

"Stay with you where?" she asked quickly.

"A hotel. We can take the bus." "Are you serious? That's it?"

"Right hand to God," Darren promised, raising his right hand.

Tamia packed a bag, Darren packed two, and fifteen minutes later they were on a CTA bus, barreling down Roosevelt Road.

Chapter 8

Suwu had driven away from the Wilkins home mere seconds before a trio of Chicago Police Department vehicles – an SUV and two patrol cars – had come speeding around the corner.

Kev sat in the backseat with the AR-15 stretched across his lap, staring vacantly out his darkly tinted window. He dared not look to his left, where Kobe was seated. He believed that he might not be able to hold back from blowing Kobe's brains all over the rear passenger compartment. Junior had been Kev's favorite younger cousin and knowing that Kobe's car was involved in Junior's murder had Kev on fifty.

"I really wish I could've went in there to see how Shawnna was doing," Kobe was saying. "Iknow she probably still hates my guts for cheating on her. Should've stuck with my first mind and just stayed in the house with her that night. Losing her trust was the biggest mistake of my life. It's like that R. Kelly song, "When A Woman's Fed Up," you know? There really ain't nothing you can do about it. It really is like running out of love."

Suwu reached a big black hand up to the rear-view mirror and angled it to Kobe's face. "Nigga," he said, "if you don't get off that emotional ass bullshit I'ma unlock your door andhave K push you out while I'm driving. A nigga just robbed his uncle. Not only his uncle, but mymothafuckin nigga. Love is the last thing on our minds right now."

"Yeah, you're right. My bad." Kobe was silent for a moment. Then he turned in his seat so he could look at Kev, his brows knitted quizzically. "I got a question. If Juice is Kev's uncle, andReese is Kev's nephew… doesn't that make it incest for Reese to be fucking with Shawnna?"

"Juice is my daddy's brother," Kev answered. "Reese is my sister's son and me and mysister have different daddies.

Therefore Reese and Shawnna are both related to me and in no wayrelated to each other."

"Speaking of Reese," Suwu said, changing to a more important topic of discussion, "he texted me right when we walked in Juice's door. Told me to ask you to come with us out to the mansion so he could talk some more with you about that deal, and when I told him what had just went down at Juice's house he said to ask you if it was that same nigga."

"More than likely it was. I can call him and ask. And *yeah*, I'll go to his mansion. What kind of question is that? Who wouldn't wanna go to a mansion?"

Kev could not believe his ears. There wasn't enough money in the world to convince him to turn against the mob and here was a guy doing just that for a measly fifty thousand dollars.

To soothe the tension, Kev picked up his Styrofoam cup of pineapple Fanta soda mixed with Actavis promethazine and codeine syrup from the cup holder and gulped down a mouthful of the narcotic beverage. Like most members of Bankroll Reese's entourage, he suffered from a strong addiction to Kush, Lean, and pain pills. The small bag of Xanax bars in his pocket was exactly what he needed to knock out all the kinks, but Xanax had a way of putting him to sleep for ten and twenty minutes at a time and he couldn't afford the luxury of napping at a time like this – he had to take care of Kobe first.

Chapter 9

Growing up in North Lawndale (or "Holy City," as the locals called it) and experiencing more drug dealing and black-on-black gun violence than any urban novel could ever accurately depict, Bankroll Reese had long ago determined that pouring his heart and soul into music was the therapy he needed to endure his rough upbringing. He and a number of his childhood friends had spent dozens of hours battling each other in lyrical ciphers that were heavily inspired by 50 Cent, who'd at the time been their favorite rapper.

Then, at age thirteen, on a love seat in his uncle Kev's basement one warm summer night, Reese had lost two precious things. The first was his virginity, consensually given to a sexy sixteen-year-old Puerto Rican and Black girl named Lisa. The second thing he lost that night was his dream of becoming a rapper. After having sex with Lisa, all he'd wanted to do was have sex with other girls, which had proven to be an easy feat. His strikingly good looks and the beefy rolls of cash his father had kept his pockets bulging with had done the trick.

However, after having recently witnessed his close friend Grindo's rise to fame as one of the Windy City's hottest new rap artists, his lyrical ambitions had returned, and with the eight-figure inheritance he'd received from his father at his disposal the odds of success were surely in his favor. Over the past four weeks he'd invested almost two hundred thousand dollars into a state- of the art recording studio at his Burr Ridge mansion. Finished just two days ago, it was the room where Bankroll Reese had been for about twelve of the past twenty-four hours.

As soon as he got home from the barber shop, he showered, ate a quick lunch of turkey sandwiches and two chocolate chip cookies, and then made a beeline for the studio where Grindo and a music engineer were patiently waiting while going over some beats. He asked the music engineer to step out of the room for a minute. He had some personal talk for Grindo, the kind of talk that could land them both in federal prison if the wrong person overheard it.

Grindo was a huge fellow, about as big and round as Miami rapper Rick Ross was before the weight loss and just as dark, with dreadlocks that went past his shoulders and a Lean habit that rivaled Reese's.

"I caught another play for you," Grindo said as Reese sat down in the swivel chair next to him. "A couple of 'em, actually. Got a rap nigga I just did a song with who wants nine of 'em, and his old man got a half a million for you if you can get him twenty blocks for twenty-five apiece. I told him I'd put the word out. I know a nigga who did some fed time with the old school cat, the one trying to get the twenty. He's certified out there in St. Louis."

Translation: Grindo knew a guy who had $500,000 for twenty kilos of cocaine, and the guy's son was looking to purchase nine kilos.

"That's what I gotta holler at you about," Reese said. "The plug might be fucked up.""Who, Juice?"

"Yeah, man. They just kicked his door in. Some nigga got whacked.""Nah. The feds?"

"Nuh uh, you misunderstood me. Some *niggas* tried to rob him. As a matter of fact, they *did* rob him. I just talked to Shawnna on the way here. She said some niggas kicked in the back door, tied up Dawn and Myesha, then put a gun to her head and made her and Juice empty the safe. One of the niggas got away with the money, but the other one got whacked. Bubbles – you remember Bubbles, don't you? That thick-ass stripper from my club?"

"How could I possibly forget a bad bitch like her?" Grindo

asked.

"Yeah, well, she hit one of the robbers with a gauge. Blew his head off. Suwu and Kev saw the body."

"You shittin' me?"

"Swear to God. I know, I couldn't believe it either. Bubbles ain't the type of girl to be onthat type of shit, but under the right circumstances I guess anybody could blow somebody's brains out. But fuck that. I haven't even got around to the craziest part of the story. Like I said, one of 'em got killed, the other one got away. You ain't gon' believe who that was."

"Who was it?" Grindo slid forward in his chair, his fat fingers clinging to the armrests. "Don't say it was that same nigga who killed my cousin Lil Dave."

Reese nodded. "Yup. It was Darren. They say he admitted to killing Juice's son while hewas there too. The nigga got balls, I'll give him that much. He knows about the bread we got on his head, yet he's still in the neighborhood, on straight-up bullshit."

"So why'd you say the plug was fucked up? He hit Juice for some birds or something?"

"All I know is that they got a dead body and about a hundred cops over there and Juice got another year and some change on parole. It might be over with for him. That means we might need to find another plug."

"Ain't that some shit?" Grindo asked, though it didn't sound like a question.

Reese gave a shout to the music engineer – a Grindo-sized white guy wearing a Cubs shirt – and LaShay, his personal assistant who was about an hour and twenty minutes late for work.Shay fetched a liter of Sprite, two pint-sized containers of Actavis, and two Styrofoam cups full of ice, while Big Bill the music engineer, sifted through a treasure trove of beats.

The Notes application on Reese's "business" iPhone had

accumulated twenty-three full songs and over seventy rap verses, all written within the past five months. He was going over theverses and sipping his Lean, occasionally looking up at Grindo, who was in the booth recording the last verse to a song they'd done together called "Drug Dealer's Dreams," when Shay walked over to him.

"I'm sorry for being so late today," she said, holding her iPad to the chest of her form-fitting black Gucci dress. "You know Bubbles is my girl. I was on my way to meet you at the barber shop when she called and told me what happened. I can't lie, I pulled over to the side of the road and cried with her for a good twenty minutes. Then I had to fix my face and get my makeup backtogether, only to get to Rev's ten minutes later and find that you had already left. And I woke up late too. This just isn't my day."

Reese looked up at her, his smile growing steadily. Though not thickly-proportioned like he preferred his women, Shay was a naturally beautiful woman, brown-skinned and modelesque with the kind of bright-spirited personality that no one could hate. Her face was sweet, her mouthwas made for a smile, and her legs went on forever.

"It's all good," Reese said, easing back in his swivel and offering her his undivided attention. "Were you able to get everything I asked you for?"

"Most of it." Shay turned on the iPad screen and went to her notes. "My first stop this morning was Tiffany's. I picked up the ring. I also got you another big box of Magnums, twelve liter-sized bottles of Sprite, your package of belts and sunglasses from Louis Vuitton, four sleeves of Styrofoam cups, five large boxes of Kellogg's Frosted Flakes, five packs of those chocolate chip cookies you can't seem to get enough of" – she sighed and shifted her weightfrom one six-inch heel to the other – "NBA 2K17 and Madden '17, four new Xbox controllers, and five fifths of Hennessy. The hair grease you wanted was out of stock; I'll order it online."

Nodding his head, Reese made a move with his right foot that sent his swivel into a slow spin.

"If you don't mind me asking," Shay said, "what are you going to do with all those condoms? Your usual stable of circus freaks has been MIA ever since Shawnna popped up on the scene. What, is she making you strap up every time? I wouldn't blame her if she did."

Reese laughed. "Circus freaks?"Shay nodded rapidly.

"You're a hater," Reese concluded.

His second iPhone rang and his uncle Kev's picture came on the screen."Lord, what it is?" he answered.

"We're down here in the garage with Kobe," Kev said.

"I'm on my way." Reese ended the call and rose to his feet. Face to face with Shay, he grinned.

She rolled her eyes.

He said, "You know that little shed out back, by the swimming pool?"She nodded.

"Go in there and look right next to that lawnmower. You should see a red container of gasoline right next to it. Grab that and one of those tall wooden chairs from the kitchen, get those furry red handcuffs off the headboard in my bedroom, and bring it all to me in the garage."

Chapter 10

Today was a day of firsts for Tamia.

Just a few hours ago, she had cheated on Kobe for the first time and she had also gotten her ass eaten for the first time. Now, lying back on Darren's chest in a king-sized bed at The Wit hotel with her knees pulled up to her ears and her mouth hanging wide open, she was for the veryfirst time experiencing anal sex. Contrary to her longstanding opinion that anal had to be painful and completely unenjoyable for the woman, she was not at all in pain and she was most certainly enjoying the experience.

They were in a room the desk clerk had described as the "Romantic Retreat Suite," an $800- a-night room that boasted mirrors on every wall, three long rectangular ceiling mirrors, and thousand-thread-count sheets. The heart-shaped lay out of red rose petals that had been on the bed when they walked in was now scattered about. One rose petal was stuck to Darren's scrotum

– Tamia could see it in the reflection of the mirror she faced – and another had somehow found its way onto her clitoris. She might have flicked it off if Darren didn't have her arms pinned backwith her legs.

Moaning and hollering like a woman giving birth to a ten-pound baby, Tamia watched the reflection of Darren's dick as it drilled her rectum, surprised at how easily something so bigcould slide in and out of her tiny little butt hole. He'd only spent a few minutes loosening her up with his tongue and two fingers. She had begged him to take it nice and slow, but he hadn'treally listened. Thirty seconds in he'd been fucking her just as hard as he was now.

"You love this shit, don't you?" he asked, breathing heavily into the crook of her neck."Yes," she panted. "Yes. Oooh, yes."

"I knew you loved it. I knew it. That pretty-boy nigga didn't know what to do with all that ass you got down there. This that gangsta-dick. It's all I got for you. It's what you needed, ain't it?"

"Yes. Mmm… mmm, yes…"

"Tell me it's what you need. Say it.""I need it."

"You need what?" Darren persisted.

"I need that gangsta dick!" Tamia shouted, louder than she'd intended to shout.

Her unintentionally loud shout was followed by another first: Tamia had an orgasm without any clitoral stimulation. She cringed and moaned and involuntarily shook as she succumbed to the most intense orgasm she'd ever had.

Darren must have been able to sense that she was coming, because at that very moment he slipped from beneath her, took off the condom, got on top of her, and parted her vaginal walls with the length of his pulsating erection.

To Tamia, who was still quivering from the effects of the explosive orgasm, being impaled by Darren's "gangsta dick" was like waking up with a growling stomach and a freezer fully of strawberry shortcake. And she absolutely loved strawberry shortcake.

Up until the minute she woke up with her legs in the air that morning, Tamia had absolutely hated Darren. A sucker for pretty boys, she had sat up in bed with Kobe many nights over the past thirty days or so complaining about his "ugly friend" who could not seem to unglue himself from her living room sofa. She'd called him "Scaren" behind closed doors and in text messagesto her friends, in reference to his scary looks. Although he had begun to wear decent outfits around the same time he had practically moved in with her and Kobe, she'd still found him to be about as visually appealing as a gargoyle with chickenpox.

Now, looking up at him with her mouth open and her hands pressed against his rib cage, while his dreadlocks swung wildly mere inches from her face as his dick went up and down in her pussy like a freshly oiled piston, she decided that he didn't look so bad. In fact, she might go as far as to start seeking out less attractive men in the immediate future. If their sex game was even half as good as Darren's, she just might fall in love.

"Here it goes," Darren said, pulling out of her and throwing himself forward so that the head of his dick was close enough to knock at her chin as he jerked his length in one hand and held her shoulder with the other. "I want you to open up that mouth for me. You want this nut in your mouth anyway. Don't you? Nasty ass."

Her mouth was already open, so she opened it a couple of inches wider. She wasn't a huge fan of catching cum in her mouth, but she didn't mind doing it from time to time. Especially when it didn't taste all funky like Kobe's sometimes did. This morning Darren's had tasted okay. There had been a lot of it – about two or three times as much as Kobe's dick usually spit out – and she was proud of herself for swallowing it all. She figured another dose of protein would go down just as smoothly. She figured wrong.

The first ribbon of semen shot into her left nostril and up to her left eye, which managed to shut just in time to avoid being blinded. The second, third, and fourth ribbons striped her face and forced her to shut her other eye. She sucked just the head of his dick into her mouth to prevent it from plastering her face any more than it already had, and what seemed like seven or eight more thick ropes of cum played target practice with her tonsils.

Having suffered enough throat torture, she took her mouth off of him and turned her head, grimacing at the mouthful of semen while Darren fired off one last shot up the side of her neck and into her right ear.

"I knew it," Darren said. "I knew you had some porn star in you. It just took a nigga like me to bring it out. Now swallow that good stuff."

"Mmmmm." She shook her head in the negative, thumbed and fingered the globs off her eyelids, and slapped his arm, urging him to unstraddle her so she could run to the bathroom.

Instead of dismounting, he pinched her nose shut and let out a laugh. She tried to swallow, but it was a failed attempt; she gagged and spit it out over the side of the bed.

"Fucking retard," Tamia muttered. She grabbed her purse and went to the bathroom to get cleaned up, closing the door behind her.

"If they charge me for this nut on the carpet," Darren shouted after her, "it's coming out of your pocket."

"I bet that's a lie. And you need to give me my money, since we're on the subject." At the bathroom sink, she turned on the hot and cold water, adjusting it to a reasonably warm temperature, cupped her hands under the faucet, and lowered her face. Once the cum was off, she used a wet wipe to clean her ear. "Don't act like you didn't hear me, Darren. I need the twenty- eight hundred for my car and that three thousand dollars you promised me."

"You gotta help me count this shit out first, but I got you."
"How much do you think it is?"

"Do you think I would need to count it if I knew that?"

"Oh." Snickering at the dumb question she'd asked, Tamia dug in her purse and found her smartphone. She had missed a call from Kobe three minutes ago. Struck by the guilt of cheating and fear of being caught, her eyes widened to the shape of saucers, and she yelled, "Darren, you'd better not tell Kobe a damned thing about this. Be quiet for a minute so I can call himback. He just called me not even five minutes ago."

She looked around the bathroom while the phone rang: a field of glossy white ceramic tiles on the floor, enhanced with inlays of small pastel-red tiles; a reversal of that scheme on the walls,a pale-red field punctuated by white inlays.

To her right a shower stall featured a frosted-gloss door in a steel frame crusted with white corrosion. Behind her lay a bathtub encircled with glass jars of unlit candles.

Kobe answered on the second ring. "Why didn't you answer your phone?" "Because I didn't hear it ringing. Must've turned off the ringer by accident.""You at home?"

"No. Why?"

"Just stay away from the apartment for the rest of the day. I don't want you around D. He just robbed the wrong nigga and I don't want you getting caught in the crossfire if they find out where he's been laying his head."

"Shit," Tamia said, putting a thumb nail between her teeth. "He… I think he might've used my car. He asked to use it to go to the store and I haven't heard from him since. I, um… had a coworker of mine come and take me to get my hair done… so I wouldn't miss my appointment."

"Okay, let me call him and – "

For some reason, Kobe was unable to complete his sentence. Tamia heard a loud smack,then a thud, then the sound of his phone clattering to the floor. An unfamiliar male's voice, simmering with aggression, said, "Bitch ass nigga!" Seconds later the call ended.

"Oh, my God," Tamia murmured as she opened the bathroom door and stepped out with her eyes still on her phone. "D, I think something just happened to Kobe. I was on the phone with him and all of a sudden – "

Now it was Tamia who didn't complete her sentence.

The hotel room's door was wide open and Darren was gone. Her one bag and his two bags were also missing, as well as the clothes she'd worn here.

Tamia snatched the blanket off of the bed and wrapped herself with it as she crossed the room to the open door. She stuck her head out into the hallway and looked both ways. There was no one in sight.

"I know that ugly motherfucker did not just play me like this," Tamia said and slammedthe door shut.

Chapter 11

It was just minutes away from four o'clock in the afternoon when the police finally allowed Juice and the girls to leave. He got in the passenger's seat of Bubbles' all-white Mercedes Benz S550 and breathed a tremendous sigh of relief as she pulled off behind Shawnna's brand-new Dodge Charger. Sitting in the back seat, Myesha had a towel-wrapped bag of ice pressed to the knot on the side of her head and she was gazing vacantly out of her window. Not a word was spoken until the revolving beacons of red and blue were no longer a presence in the rear-view mirror.

"So," Bubbles said, breaking the silence and glancing over at Juice, "are we following the twins to Reese's mansion after we drop Myesha off?"

"You don't have to. I'll get in the car with them at Myesha's. You can go on home and watch your shows on Netflix," Juice said, typing in numbers on his smartphone's calculator to see exactly how much cash he had left altogether after the huge loss he'd taken in the robbery.

"Let me know when you're done using that calculator," Bubbles said. "I need you to calculate some shit for me."

"Calculate what?"

"I'll wait for you to finish." Her high-pitched tone of voice made it obvious that her intentwas less than innocent.

Juice paid it no mind. He subtracted 81,500 from 574,000 and found that he was down to

$492,500.00 which included the $2,500.00 he had in his pocket."Okay." He turned to Bubbles. "I'm done."

"Put in ten thousand, plus twelve million, multiplied by four.""You're just saying numbers."

"No, I'm not."

"What are these numbers for?"

"Ten thousand is the level of fucked-up I'm on after having to shoot somebody with a fucking shotgun. Twelve million is equivalent to just how fucked up you got me if you think

you're getting out of this car when I drop off Myesha. And you can multiply that by how many times I'm going to bust you upside your fucked up head if you so much as reach for that door latch."

Myesha laughed in the backseat.

"Damn." Juice chuckled once. "That's fucked up."

"You are not about to just leave like that," Bubbles said. "I'll be curled up in bed crying every time I think about what I had to do to that boy."

"Hell, I don't know why," Myesha said. "That 'boy' was going to rape me."

"He was so little," Bubbles said, shaking her head. "He couldn't have been older than fifteen."

Juice had no sympathy for the kid. In his opinion, anybody who was old enough to put on a mask and carry out an armed robbery was old enough to get shot. He felt vulnerable without his pistol on him. There were gang wars raging all over the city of Chicago and riding around without a gun – or "lacking," as most urban Chicagoans were fond of calling it – could very easily lead to an early grave.

He reclined his seat as far back as it could go. "That nigga admitted to killing my son," he said, gritting his teeth and balling his left hand into a fist. His right hand tightened around his phone.

"Does anybody know where he lives?" Bubbles asked. "Or where he used to live? Where he's from? Anything?"

"Thirteenth and Sawyer," Juice said. "He used to live in an apartment with his grandfather over there, but ain't nobody seen him lately. He's laying low. He knows that we know it was himand Big Jay who killed Lil Dave."

"And now he knows that you know it was him who killed Junior. He'll really be hiding out now."

"He didn't expect for you to scare his name out of his partner with that shotgun," Juice said. "It's all good, though. I'm glad this shit happened today. Now I know who killed my son. That's the only information I've been looking for. I don't even give a fuck about the money he took. It was worth losing it all to hear what he was stupid enough to tell me. Dumb ass nigga just dug hisown grave."

Bubbles parted her lips to speak, but then her phone rang. She put it to her ear. " Girl, what the hell do you want?"

With the windows up and no music playing, it was fairly easy to hear the girl's voicethrough Bubbles' iPhone: "I need you to come and pick me up as soon as possible."

"I'm not gonna be able to do that," Bubbles said as she hung a hard right onto Homan Avenue and brought the long white Mercedes to a stop in front of Myesha's bungalow home. "You know I love you and would do anything in the world for you, lil cousin, but not today. Ijust had to shoot somebody. It was in self-defense and the police cleared me of any wrongdoing, but I honest-to-God just killed somebody, okay? So you're gonna have to call somebody else to pick you up."

"You don't understand. You *have* to come and get me. The only other person I can call ismy boyfriend and he's not gonna be my man anymore if he…"

Juice tuned out the conversation as his own iPhone rang. It was Kev."You good, Unc?" Kev asked.

"Yeah, I'm good. They took my shotgun for evidence. That's about it. We blamed the chopper shells on the back porch on the robbers. Cops could tell we made that shit up but they knew they wouldn't be able to prove it."

"They let you leave yet?"

"Yup. A couple of minutes ago. We're dropping Myesha off now, then we'll be on our way to wherever y'all at. Shawnna wants to stay with Reese and you know Dawn's not leaving her side."

"Okay, hurry up. We're here at the mansion, in the basement garage. It's me, Reese, Chubb, and Suwu."

"What about Kobe?" Juice asked, making a fist with his left hand again."Oh, yeah. We got his ass right here too."

"Don't let him leave."

"He'll be here," Kev said. "I can guarantee you that."

"A'ight, I'll text you when we get there." Juice ended the call and looked over at Bubbles, who had already ended her call and was looking at him.

Myesha was out of the car and climbing the stairs to her home.

"You're not going to believe this," Bubbles said, shaking her head."What?"

"I just heard you say something about Kobe. Well, my aunt Gabby's daughter is his girlfriend and I guess she just cheated on him with some nigga who promised to give her something like six grand to give him some pussy. Long story short, they fucked at some hotel downtown and he left without paying when she went to the bathroom. He took all her clothes with him too. So now she's butt naked in that hotel room with nothing but her phone and her purse. She needs me to pick her up and bring her an outfit to wear home."

Juice managed a laugh as Bubbles pulled off behind the twins.

"That nigga Chris Brown was not lying," she said. "These hoes ain't loyal." "It must run in the family," Juice said and grinned.

Bubbles punched him in the shoulder.

Chapter 12

Darren tipped the Jamaican cab driver an extra twenty for the time he'd waited outside a luggage shop on Michigan Avenue while Darren went inside and purchased a suitcase with wheels, then he ended the cab ride at a west side used car dealership.

He walked into the dealership and was immediately greeted by a chunky saleswoman. "Good afternoon," she said. "May I show you something?"

"I'd like to see a list of every car in stock that's ready to drive away," he said.

The saleswoman went to her desk, offered him a chair, took a sip of water from a clear glass, and pulled an inventory list from a drawer. She removed a page from the list and handed it to him. "That's everything on the lot," she said. "A couple need prepping before they go out."

Darren ran down the list and stopped at a green Camaro SS. "I'll take a look at this one," he said.

"It's right over there," the woman said, pointing across the showroom. "You've got great taste in vehicles. That's a twenty-eleven model. I have the twenty-ten myself."

"I like fast cars," he replied.

"We've got a new shipment of them coming in Monday," the woman said, "so I can offeryou a good deal on that one."

Darren went over to the car and got behind the wheel. "Is it prepped to go?""Ready to drive away."

He got out of the car and checked the equipment list.

"Just about every option," the saleswoman said. "Do you have a trade-in?"

"No, just cash," he said, producing his ID and a five-thousand-dollar bundle of fifties as they returned to her desk. "Can we hurry this up? I have an important job interview to be at in less than an hour. Here is five thousand dollars. You can set up whatever kind of payment system you want to, but I'll have the car paid off in the next month or two."

"That'll be fine. Let me speak to our finance guy." She got up and walked into a private office with the cash and his ID. Five minutes later, she was back.

The printer on the woman's desk began to spit paper.

"That's the bill of sale printing out right now." She handed it to him and thanked him for hisbusiness.

A man in coveralls appeared and drove the car out of the showroom and onto the lot. Twenty minutes after arriving, Darren had become the owner of a sweet green 2011 Camaro.

He stuffed his pockets full of cash from the suitcase, put his Ruger pistol and the Glock he'd taken from Juice in the waistline of his sweats, and picked up the smartphone, which had beenoff since he abandoned Tamia at the hotel. Unsurprisingly, he had numerous voice mails and text messages from Tamia's cell phone, as well as two additional voice mails from what must have been the hotel room phone. He blocked both numbers and deleted the messages without even reading or listening to them, then gave his close friend and fellow gang member Big Jay a call.

"What's up, G?" Big Jay answered."Where you at?"

"At the grocery store with Tracy. Had to grab some hot wings and beer for the Bears game tomorrow. I bought a Link card with some of that money you gave me. Card had twelve hundredon it. We got food for days." Big Jay's guttural laugh ensued.

"Man, you know that lil nigga RoRo I had with me the other day?""Yeah. What about him?"

"I think he might be dead, G.""Why you say that?"

"We went over there and hit Juice. I got away with the bread, but RoRo didn't make it out with me," Darren explained. "I heard a loud-ass gunshot right after he shouted my name – hewas upstairs, I was downstairs. The shit sounded like a shotgun. Either that or a .50-cal. I alreadyhad the money, so I took off. Juice shot up the car as I was speeding off through the alley."

"What car? And why in the fuck would you let that nigga live?"

"I just wanted to get away with the money first. I didn't wanna let off no shots and have the police everywhere. Tamia let me use her car." Darren laughed repeatedly as he recounted the story of what went down between him and Tamia after the robbery. "I just blocked her number before I called you."

"You ain't shit, G."

"Fuck that thot. I told you how the bitch was treating me, looking at me like I had Ebola or some shit. And Kobe gave me the okay to fuck that bitch, so I fucked the bitch. Off her, though. You think I need to be worried about Juice? Think I need to shoot up his crib, run him off the west side?"

"Run him off the west side?" Big Jay echoed incredulously. "Nigga, do you hear yourself? Juice *is* the west side. At least this summer he is. Every gram of dope on the streets is coming from him. We gotta whack that nigga, G. My girl just told me she heard he got fifty racks on our heads. That means every Traveler and every Four Corner Hustler in Holy City is out looking for us. I'm staying in the house for now, or at least until I find somebody who'll let me use their car. Standing outside on Sawyer is like committing suicide. Especially when we barely even got pistols."

"I got a gun for you. Got a car we can drive too," Darren said, adding pressure to the gas pedal as he zipped through a yellow light on Chicago Avenue. "I just bought a Camaro."

"You serious?"

"On Black Gangsta," Darren swore."Nigga, come get me."

"I'm on my way. And I think I know how to find Juice."

"How?" Big Jay asked.

"You remember Myesha? The stripper? She was there when we kicked the door in at Juice's house. She lives on Homan, and she's always hanging with Dawn and Shawnna. All we gotta do is follow her. I can almost guarantee she'll lead us right to Juice."

Chapter 13

When Kobe regained consciousness he realized that his plan to betray the Black Gangsters' top enforcers for his own financial gain had failed miserably. His hands were restrained behind his back and he was seated upright in a chair of some kind. His ankles were bound to the chair, and there was a dark cloth or garment tied around his head to prevent him from seeing whatever there was to be seen. Moving his tongue around in his mouth, he found that several of his teeth were either broken or missing, and he tasted blood. His head and chest throbbed with pain, and his entire body was soaking wet. In a terrifying combination of fear and panic, he began to cry. Which was when someone behind the chair snatched the blinding cloth off his head.

He was sitting in the middle of Bankroll Reese's underground parking garage, an enormous room that seemed to be made entirely of white marble and was lined on both sides with Bentleys,Roll-Royces, Lamborghinis, Ferraris, and Mercedes Benzes. There were five people standing five feet in front of him. From left to right they were Bankroll Reese, Kev, Juice, Shawnna, and Dawn, and all of them were scowling at him as though they had captured a neighborhood rapist. Reese was lighting a blunt, Kev was puffing on another blunt, both of them had Styrofoam cups in their left hands. In one hand Juice held a cigarette lighter, and the fingers of his other hand were gripped tight around the wooden handle of a sledgehammer.

Kobe's sobbing intensified when the stench of the gasoline he was soaked in finally hit him.

"Of all the cameras on Sixteenth Street," Juice said, slowly walking toward Kobe, "only three of them actually work. Now, one of those belongs to the Chicago Police Department, so I can't possibly know what that one sees. But then there's the other two." Juice lifted the hammer high above his head and brought it down hard.

"No, no, no, please!" Kobe said quickly and squeezed his eyes shut as the sledgehammer hit his left thigh and crushed his femur bone.

His ear-piercing scream was more like a howl. Juice stood over him, showing not even the slightest trace of sympathy as Kobe screamed again, and again.

"You see," Juice went on, "those other two cameras belong to Rev and my young homie Reese, both of whom are *great* friends of mine."

"Shawnna!" Kobe cried out to his ex-girlfriend. "Baby, *please*!"

"Don't call on me after you done played a part in my brother getting killed!" Shawnna snapped.

"Now," Juice continued, circling the chair and dragging the sledgehammer along behind him, "Rev's camera can't really see much aside from who's coming and going at his barber shop,but the camera system at Reese's strip club is top-notch. That motherfucker can look east, west –it can zoom in, zoom out. And guess whose car it caught pulling up next to the Cadillac I had justgiven to my son?"

"It was Darren and RoRo," Kobe said, sobbing uncontrollably. "I didn't know, I swear to God, I didn't know."

Juice stopped in front of Kobe. "Where can I find Darren and RoRo? Huh? Speak fast,nigga. My patience is thin."

"At my girl's apartment. They was there when I left. Please, man. I loved Junior. Y'all know

I – "

Juice raised the sledgehammer a second time and Kobe jerked away so hard that the chair

tipped over backward. Everyone laughed – everyone but Kobe.

"At Tamia's apartment?" Juice asked, lowering the sledge-hammer back to his side.

Kobe nodded vehemently while a part of his mind wondered how Juice had learned Tamia's name. "Please don't hit me with that hammer again. You broke my leg, man. I can't feel my shit. Please, just let me go. I swear to God, man, I won't tell nobody about this shit. Just let me go home. Y'all ain't gotta kill me, G. I'm a real nigga. Y'all know me. I ain't never did y'allwrong."

"Unc," Kev said, "did that nigga just call you a G?"

"Killed his damned self," Juice said, shaking his head as he struck a flame and lit Kobe's shirt ablaze. "Called me a G. Nigga, I'm a Vice Lord."

Kobe began scream-howling again as his entire body went up in flames.

Chapter 14

"Five minutes my ass," Bubbles said as Juice lowered himself back down into the passenger's seat of her Mercedes.

Already smiling, he pulled the door shut and turned to her. "What was that you just said about your ass?" he asked. "I can only get five minutes with it? Fuck it, I'll take that."

She rolled her eyes and smirked, then shifted into drive and stomped on the gas, propelling the luxury sedan out of the Villa Taj's driveway. "Why do you have to be such a perv?" she asked.

"Why do you have to look so sexy? That's the better question.""Good game, D. Wade."

"That ain't game. It's the truth."

"Whatever, Juice. Believe me, working the pole at Redbone's, I have literally heard every line out there, and I can see through every bit of it. The fact of the matter is, if I didn't have all this ass, niggas would not be checking for me. All you niggas want to do is fuck a bad bitch with a big booty. That shit was cool when I was younger, but now I'm almost thirty and I got a daughter to raise. I'm trying to travel the world and buy properties. Most niggas are too broke and simple-minded to understand that kinda mindset."

"I understand it very well. You got one daughter; I have two grown daughters who are very expensive to take care of and I've taken good care of them ever since they were born. Even when I was in prison, I made sure they always had the stuff they needed. That goes for the twins and my son. Oh, and for the record, I'm nothing like those bums you see at the strip club every night,throwing their last two or three hundred every other weekend. I'm a big dog. I might not travel but I'm a Traveler. I might not own a bunch of properties but I run a whole neighborhood. The only reason I go to that strip club is to see you."

"Mmm hmm. It sounds good," Bubbles said.

"You're the sexiest girl I've ever seen up close," Juice said. "Woman," she corrected.

"Sexiest woman," he said. "You know what I meant."

"I know, but there's a difference. And speaking of money, how much did you lose in that robbery?"

"Eighty-one five."

"Eighty-one thousand and five hundred dollars?"

Juice nodded. "It ain't shit, though. I'll make it back in one play."

"Earlier," Bubbles said, "when all of that went down, I kept trying to remember where I'd heard the name Darren before. It just hit me: Brianna, one of the girls I work with at Redbone's, was in her car on Sixteenth and Drake when Lil Dave got killed, and she said it was Darren and some guy named Big Jay who did it. She told the police that it was Big Jay who shot Lil Dave and that other boy, but when she got jumped by some girls in the club for snitching she changed her story and went down to Georgia. I heard she's stripping at Kamal's in Atlanta now. Not sure how true it is. Big Jay's double-murder charges got dismissed. From what I've heard, Big Jay and Darren are like brothers. If you can find one, you'll more than likely find the other one right there with him."

Bubbles glanced at her phone as it started ringing. She ignored the call and lifted her eyes back to the road.

"Why do you keep ignoring your calls?" Juice asked. She gave him a quizzical look. "What?"

"Don't play dumb. You know what I'm talking about. That's the second time you didn't answer your phone in front of me. Who is that, your boyfriend or somebody?"

"I told you, I don't have a boyfriend."

"Well, who is it? Stop dodging the question." "I'm not

dodging the question."

"Then answer it."

Bubbles sighed and kept her attention on the road ahead. "Never mind," Juice said. "Forget I even asked."

"He's not my boyfriend," Bubbles said. "He's just a rich nigga who thinks that just becausehe's rich and famous he can have me as his side chick whenever his wife gets on his nerves."

"Can I get a name?"

"It's Blake, the rapper everybody knows as Bulletface."

"Whaaat?!" Juice exclaimed. He'd heard all about the billionaire rap mogul's fling with Bubbles, but to actually witness proof of it was shocking. His brows rose high on his forehead as it all registered in his brain. "Damn, that's crazy. Do you know how many women would kill to have that nigga call their phone? Most females would divorce their husbands."

"I'm different from most females."

"Bulletface is the reason Cup was so rich. They kidnapped his daughter and made him pay something like fifty million to get her back. That's how Reese was able to inherit all thatmoney."

"I know all about it," Bubbles said. "Blake's the reason I moved here to Chicago and started working at Redbone's in the first place. He wanted me to find out who had kidnapped his daughter. He ended up finding out that it was Cup, but by then he was making so much money with Cup's gang that he decided not to do anything about it and I was making so much money at the strip club that I decided to just stay here in the city. He bought me a yellow Lamborghini and a house in New York a while back, but after his psychotic wife had *me* kidnapped last year, I sold all that shit, bought myself a bigger place here in Chicago, and put the rest in the bank. Haven't given him the time of day ever since."

"Then why does he keep calling you?" Juice asked, becoming more and more intrigued by the second.

"Because," Bubbles replied, "like most men in the rap game, he wants to plunge in and out of as many big-bootied bad bitches as he possibly can. But, little does he know, Lakita Thomas ain't going for it no more. I don't even want to *see* another rapper. That nigga made me quit even listening to rap music. If it's not R&B, I don't wanna hear it."

Ever resourceful, Juice thumbed his way to the Pandora app on his iPhone and hit *play* on the R. Kelly station. Two seconds later "Honey Love" began to play and he upped the volume.

Bubbles threw her head back and laughed. "You are too slick for me," she said."We on our way to pick up your cousin from the hotel?" Juice asked.

"No. My mom picked her up. They're at my place. I hope you like to play spades. It's what my family likes to do on most Friday nights."

"Deal me in," Juice said.

Chapter 15

Lakita Thomas took off her robe and looked at herself in the full-length mirror. "Twenty- five-inch hips," she said. "Not bad."

Her closet was as big as a master bedroom and there was a second one just like it. This closet was for daytime wear. She walked through the racks of dresses and pulled out a Dolce & Gabbana stretch leather mini – strawberry red. The peep toe pumps she selected were Prada, and when she finished dressing, she took another look in the mirror. Juice would be speechless. He was in the living room with her mother, Linda Cambridge, and her cousin Tamia.

Situated in the heart of Lake Forest, Illinois, Lakita's swanky 5,059-square-foot home had 30-foot ceilings in the living room and an English basement with a dance studio, art studio, and kitchen. The property had a greenhouse – 59-by-22-feet with a stone walkway, a koi pond, and an attached octagonal sitting room – a gazebo, and a shared 2-acre lake and it abutted an 800- acre forest preserve. With four bedrooms, four and a half bathrooms, and a four-car garage, the home had cost Lakita a cool $1.65 million.

Her twelve-year-old daughter Ra'Mya was lying across her huge bed when she camesauntering out of the closet. "Oh, my God," Ra'Mya said, sitting up Indian-style. "Hashtag, mom goals. Hashtag, booty goals. Hashtag, body goals. Hashtag, all kinds of goals."

Lakita put her hands on her hips and smiled. "All jokes aside. How do I look?""Like the queen of all thots."

"Don't get strangled."

Ra'Mya laughed. "You look amazing like always, Mom. I don't even know why you asked. The boys would go berserk if I posted a pic of you on my Snapchat. Like, seriously. I hope I can look like you when I'm old."

"I'm not old."

"Who's that bald-headed man? Where'd you meet him?"

"His name's Juice. Remember when we went to that football game with the twin girls?" "Yeah, and that big boy who played on the team got a ride home with us."

"Those are Juice's kids."

"Dang, that means he's older than you, huh? No wonder he's bald.""Call me old again and see if – "

"Hashtag, elderly gang."They both laughed.

"I can't with you," Lakita/Bubbles said, shaking her head.

"Okay. No more jokes for now," Ra'Mya said. "Seriously, though – why are you all dressed up? Is he taking you out on a date? I could've sworn you told me we were all gonna stay in and play Spades tonight."

"I'm not going out. We are gonna play Spades." "Dressed like that?"

"What's wrong with this?"

"Mom, you absolutely positively cannot be serious." Ra'Mya closed her eyes, pinched the bridge of her nose between her thumb and forefinger, and pointed her other forefinger at the closet Lakita had emerged from a moment ago. "I want you to go back in there and find yourself a casual T-shirt and a nice pair of sweatpants, leggings, or pajama pants. Either that or I'll be forced to kick you and to get hauled off to jail for mom abuse."

Chapter 16

Lee Wilkins Sr. was seeing dollar signs. Ever since Bubbles had mentioned Bulletface's business relations with Cup, all Juice had been able to think about were the millions of dollars he himself would make if he were ever to get the same drug connect. Cup had left well over fifty million dollars and a string of popular nightclubs to his son; Juice wanted to leave his twin girls with at least a couple of million.

Judging from the sheer size and grandeur of the suburban home Bubbles had just brought him to, he figured that she too had made off good from her relationship with Bulletface. He madea mental note to bring up the topic again later on tonight. Maybe she would be able to plug him in with the Grammy-award-winning rap superstar, who could then plug him in with someMexican drug lord with the resources to take over the city.

Now, as he sat in the middle of a tan leather sofa, in the living room of a house that was about five times bigger than his own, he shifted his thoughts to a more pressing matter.

Tamia was sitting next to him, doing ten different things at once on her iPhone, with one socked foot pulled up on the sofa with her. She was a pretty girl, short and nimble, and just like her cousin Bubbles she had a peanut butter complexion and a huge butt.

"You don't even remember me, do you?" Juice said, nudging her with an elbow.She looked at him. "Am I supposed to?"

"You're the same age as my daughters. You all played together when they were like one ortwo years old, back when we all lived on Trumbull."

"Wow, really? I know that's where we stayed when I was born, but I honestly don'tremember any of it."

"I wanted to ask you something."

"Ask away," she said, already back on her phone. "You

know somebody named Darren?"

Tamia put down her phone and flicked her eyes over at Juice; the rising anger in them was palpable. "Yeah, I know him," she said coldly. "He's the same bitch-made nigga who left me stuck at that hotel today. Mind you, this is after I let him sleep on my couch every night for the past month or so because his punk ass was too scared to go home. I let him use my car this morning and when he brought it back the damned thing was all shot up. He was supposed to pay me twenty-eight hundred for it but he didn't. All he did was take me to the hotel. Then he took all my stuff and left while I was in the bathroom." She balled up her fists and made an angry growling sound in her throat. "I swear, I could kill that bitch."

"You know where to find him?"

"I wouldn't be sitting here if I did."

"Just think about it for a minute. You gotta know some way to find him.""He blocked my phone number, so I can't – "

"You got his phone number?"

She nodded yes, then regarded Juice with questioning eyebrows.

"Here." He produced a wad of cash and peeled off a hundred. "I'll give you a hundred forthat number."

"You want his phone number so bad that you're willing to pay a hundred dollars for it?" Shetook the bill and folded it into her palm. "Not that I'm complaining about it."

She gave him the number verbally and he saved it in his smartphone. "Anything else you can think of?" he asked, still holding the cash.

"He blocked me on Instagram and I don't think he has a Facebook page."

Just when Juice was fixing his mouth to ask another question, Bubbles' mom shouted that the pizza Bubbles ordered half an hour ago had arrived and two seconds later Bubbles and her daughter walked into the living room dressed similarly in T-shirts and sweatpants, which wasalso what Tamia had on. It surprised Juice just how much Ra'Mya's facial features resembled her mother's. He'd thought the same of Bubbles when he first walked in and saw Linda mopping the kitchen floor.

Bubbles gave Ra'Mya three twenty-dollar bills and sent her and Tamia to get the boxes of pizza, bread sticks, and wings and two-liter bottles of Sprite and Pepsi from the Pizza Hut deliveryman. She then told Juice to follow her downstairs to the basement.

"It's where the card table is set up," she explained.

Juice did not really need the explanation. With the way her ass wobbled and bounced in the white sweatpants as she sauntered off toward the rear of the house, Juice would have followedher anywhere.

She wore tall white heels with red bottoms – Christian Louboutins – and they click-clacked steadily across the hardwood floors as she led the way to the basement door, which was open when they reached it.

He very badly wanted to reach out and fill his hands with her ass, but she reached back and took his hand, leading him down into the dark basement, which smelled of stone, old wood, and paint. She had no trouble negotiating the space in the darkness, which led him to believe she'd performed this drill many times before. Why? Had she been bringing other guys down here inthe dark? Guys she'd met at the strip club? Was she lying about not having had sex in over a year?

Thoughts stuck in his mind like thorns he couldn't reach. They had stopped in front of what seemed to be a solid stone wall. He reached out, confirmed his supposition. All at once, a light came on. He saw on the stone wall that Bubbles must have flipped up.

"The switch at the top of the stairs is broken," she said and they continued on through the stone-walled basement.

"I'll fix it for you," Juice said. "I became a certified electrician in prison. Took the three- month class for a six-month time cut."

"Uh-oh." She smirked. "Got myself a handyman." "Fuck outta here."

"What? There's nothing wrong with being a handyman." "I'm sure you have a long line of handymen."

"Well," she said, leading him into a kitchen, "you're wrong. You can ask Ra'Mya, there hasn't been a man in this house since the movers brought in my furniture."

There was an ashtray and a deck of playing cards on an old-fashioned folding bridge table. Four metal folding chairs were pulled up to the table. Juice took the chair that would put his backto the wall, while Bubbles set her purse on the seat of the chair directly across from him and thenwent to a stainless steel refrigerator and took out an ice tray.

"Do me a huge favor," she said. "Take the idea of me being a stripper out of your mind for the time being. And don't call me Bubbles in front of my family. Call me Lakita or Kita."

"I can do that."

"You sure about that?"

"Yeah. What's so hard about calling you a different name?"

"No, not the name part. I mean can you stop thinking of me as a stripper? I feel like it puts you in a mind of me being a whore. What I am is a professional exotic dancer who works to take care of her child like every other responsible mother. Don't let my job define me. That's one of the many reasons I've been celibate for so long."

Her intuition couldn't have possibly been more accurate. He realized that, somewhere in the back of his mind, he had already labeled her a promiscuous woman. Like most men he knew, he'd always viewed strippers as money-hungry gold-diggers who would fuck any man or womanwith a pocketful of cash. He believed there had to be a ton of truth to the whole strippers-are- sluts theory, but he couldn't throw them all in the same box. If he did that he would be no different than the cops who treated all Blacks like criminals.

Lakita's mom didn't join the Spades party. Ra'Mya and Tamia teamed up against Lakita andJuice, but not before all of them scarfed down the pizza. Ra'Mya fetched a Beats by Dre Pill speaker and played a mix featuring tracks from Future, Chance the Rapper, Drake, Fetty Wap, Bulletface, Yo Gotti, and Dreezy, among others. Lakita pulled a bottle of Hennessy from the freezer and filled red plastic tumblers for herself, Tamia, and Juice.

Every time a Bulletface song played, Juice thought of the phone calls Lakita had ignored in his presence. Bulletface was reportedly worth more than a billion and a half dollars and his wife, Alexus Costilla, was currently tied with Bill Gates with a net worth of $79 billion. Juice had Googled the celebrity couple's net worths during the drive out to Lake Forest.

They were just starting the second game when the sound of the doorbell ringing put an end to things. Apparently, Ra'Mya was having a sleepover and her friends arrived at a few minutes past eight. She abandoned the table and ran upstairs, shouting for her older cousin to come with her.

"Here I come!" Tamia shouted back, swallowing the last of her drink as she stood up. "Don't you go up there acting all drunk in front of those girls," Lakita said tightly. "Girl, I got this," Tamia shot back.

"No sex talk."

"You don't think I know that?"

"I'm for real, Mia. Keep it cute."

"I'm not drunk, Kita. A little tipsy, maybe, but definitely

not drunk.""One complaint from the girls and I'm sending you home."

"You do remember that I'm grown now, right?" Tamia asked, leaving the kitchen. Amoment later, they could hear her stomping her way up the stairs.

A sneaky, conspiratorial grin stretched across Juice's face as he moved back in his chair with his cup of iced cognac in hand.

"Don't look at me that way." Lakita smirked. "You creep."
"Everything happens for a reason," Juice said.

"Oh, please."

"God's will."

"Shut up."

"All the stars are aligned."

"You are so full of shit," Lakita said, laughing merrily as she got up and refilled their cups. "Don't forget about the blunt and that bag of weed and pills you stuffed in my purse before the police got there."

"Damn, I had forgot all about that. Fire up that blunt." Juice's eyes were fastened to Lakita's hip-hugging sweatpants. It was no wonder she had a billionaire rap star on her heels. She possessed the body of an African goddess, the kind of body some women nowadays paid tens of thousands of dollars to get, and she had the beautiful face to match.

"We're not smoking in the house," she said, picking up her purse and the Hennessy bottle. "Come on, we're going up to my room to watch *Narcos*. If you wanna smoke you can go outsideand sit in the car."

"Shit, fuck that weed. *Narcos* it is."

Feeling slightly buzzed and very aroused, Juice followed Lakita back up the stairs. This time he didn't hold back form smacking and squeezing her thick derriere cheeks and she didn't seem to mind at all.

Chapter 17

With the sun gone from the sky, Darren felt relatively comfortable driving down 16th Street. He had his Ruger on his lap. Seated next to him was Big Jay and on Big Jay's lap lay the Glock that had belonged to Juice. Their faces mostly hidden behind long dreadlocks, the two ruthless gang members were on the hunt. They were hoping to catch an enemy lacking on this warm summer night.

"G, a nigga gotta get it tonight," Big Jay said, looking left and right and then over his shoulder. "We ain't gon' be able to just wait on that bitch Myesha to come out and lead us to Juice. These niggas are out here looking for us at the same time we're looking for them. Can't let them hit us up before we can hit them."

"I already know, G." Darren's eyes were peeled for any signs of gang activity. He'd passed a large group of gang members a few blocks back, but all of them were youngsters, many of them hardly even teens, and he wanted to get somebody higher up, somebody the Vice Lords and Four Corner Hustlers would really be upset about losing.

Big Jay used the Glock to point at a car they were approaching. Darren was already on it. Parked in front of the barber shop was Kobe's white Chevy Caprice, its over-sized chrome rims glistening in the reflection of headlights.

They had to pause and wait for the slow crawl of vehicles backed up along the street to move forward. The air was stifling with the accumulation of exhaust fumes. People were everywhere: Black girls in twos, fours, and larger groups, some in line to get into Redbone's, others mingling on the street corners; a squad of Black teenage boys at the opening of the alleyway, swapping drugs for cash and watching out for cops; exasperated drivers and passengers sticking their heads out of windows to see what the traffic jam was all about. An older man walked up to Darren's window and said "Loose squares, loose squares, loose squares for sale," and he brought with him the putrid stench of crack smoke, questionable body odor, andcheap cologne.

The traffic flow sped up a bit and Darren was driving past Kobe's car when something caught his eye. The Chevy Caprice's trunk was open and a light skinned man was stuffing ablack garbage bag into it. A large Bentley sedan was parked behind the Caprice. Darren stomped down on the brakes when he realized that the man was Kev, Juice's nephew and the second in command for the brand of Vice Lords that were after Darren and Big Jay.

"That's Kev right there," Darren said, getting ready to lift his gun and open fire.

But Big Jay stopped him. "Let me get this nigga up-close," Big Jay said. "Just be ready to pull off. This for sis."

Big Jay's fifteen-year-old sister had been shot and killed while standing outside with friends on 13th and Sawyer one fateful evening two months ago, which was why he'd sent two boys – Head and Lil Dave – to their graves in a hail of bullets shortly after her funeral.

Darren's eyeballs darted around in their sockets as Big Jay threw open the passenger's side door and got out. To be so wide and lanky, Big Jay moved rather swiftly, like a retired running back who'd gained eighty pounds since leaving the league but still had what it took to make a triumphant return to the field. Kev had just slammed the trunk shut when Big Jay raised the Glock and started firing. Calmly, with a kind of serene confidence, he squeezed off three-four- five shots. They all seemed to hit Kev, who fell to the ground and went scrambling around the side of the Caprice. The large window at the front of Rev's Barber Shop was struck by a bullet; itshattered, sending glass raining down onto the sidewalk. Big Jay continued forward, determined to finish the job, impervious to the screams of women as people began running for their lives.

Explosions of even louder gunshots immediately followed and it took a few seconds for Darren to realize that the Bentley's driver's door was open and the man standing behind it – a man as tall and broad-shouldered as Big Jay – was firing round after round into Big Jay's back.

Acting on what could have been nothing but pure survival instinct, Big Jay took one giant leap toward the Camaro and dove in through the passenger's door, which he'd wisely left open. Without a moment's hesitation Darren whipped up the Ruger and shot three times through the rear passenger's side window. They all struck the Bentley driver's door within six inches of one another and sent the big man ducking into the quarter-million-dollar car.

Amid an outraged bray of horns and squeals of tires Darren turned left onto the Trumbull Avenue alleyway. He mowed down one of the teenage drug dealers and didn't flinch when his car tires bumped over the body.

"G… I'm hit, G! He shot me!"

"I know. Just try to breathe," Darren said without looking at his wounded friend. "I'm about to get you to a hospital. Just stay with me. Don't close your eyes. Breathe and keep your eyes open and keep talking to me."

He left the alleyway with a hard right turn onto 15th Street, stopped just long enough to getBig Jay's door shut, and then stomped the gas pedal back down to the floorboard.

Chapter 18

"I swear, when I first started watching this show, I didn't have a clue who Pablo Escobar was," Bubbles said, looking at the seventy-inch flat-screen television on the wall across from her king-size bed.

She was being funny. There was no way Juice could pay attention to the TV. As soon as they'd entered her bedroom, she had locked the door and said "Okay, you can think of me as Bubbles now." Then she'd told him to strip down to his underwear and make himself at home while she went into her bathroom to freshen up. She had just returned wearing nothing but her diamond jewelry and her snow-white Louboutin heels.

Juice lay in bed in a black pair of boxer shorts, his mouth and eyes stretched wide as he tookin the glorious sight before him. The silver TV remote in his hand was the tool he'd used to restart the fourth episode of her favorite Netflix show. An intoxicated grin appeared on his face. "Damn," he muttered breathlessly.

"I have a stripper pole in my closet," Bubbles said. "I can set it up right here at the foot ofthe bed, if you want me to. Give you a private dance show, you know?"

He shook his head emphatically. "I got all the pole you need. Get over here and quit teasing me."

"Look at you. Old horny ass." "Ain't no need to look at me."

"I think we should watch at least a couple of episodes of old Pablo first," Bubbles said as she climbed onto the bed, turned so that her side was to him, and started moving her bountiful buttocks one cheek at a time. It was a trick she'd learned during her first few weeks at Redbone's.

"Motherfuck Pablo." Juice hit the power button on the remote. The TV went black as he leaned forward and, curling his fingers around her forearm, said in a low voice, "I am going to fuck the life out of you, Bubbles."

His eyes sought hers, engaged them as he pulled her onto his lap. In his gaze were all the memories of their shared past, all the private dances she'd given him at the strip club, all the times he'd dreamed of making love to her, all the fantasies she'd starred in. To him, her sweet brown eyes were like a looking glass in which he saw the best of himself being given to the mostbeautiful woman he'd ever encountered.

"You ready for it?" he asked with lust in his tone.

She nodded, but she wasn't so sure. It had been so long since she'd given herself to a man that she was leery of going through with it. Her pulse was heavy in the side of her neck. His fingertips on her carotid picked up the throb as if it were a seismic shift.

"Is this how you are when you're about to have sex?" he asked softly.

Mutely, she nodded her head again, biting her bottom lip and placing her hands on his strongshoulders. She felt his dick rising to attention beneath her as he took a breast in his mouth and administered several sharp smacks to her ass, smacks that made her gasp involuntarily and sent her vaginal juices to churning.

He did a slow roll that put him on top and her at the bottom. He had a bit of a gut, but it wasn't a turn-off. If anything it was a turn-on. Bubbles liked her men tall and meaty and also well-endowed. Judging from the way his erection had his boxer shorts sticking out at the crotch, the latter of her likes was more than accounted for. His mouth moved from one breast to the other. Her hands went to the sides of his head and she pressed her fingers tight against hissmooth hairless scalp as he kissed his way down to her pulsating clitoris and, unhesitatingly, began flicking the pointed tip of his tongue on and around it. He pushed his tongue inside as deep as it could possibly go, then went to sucking and nibbling gently on her clit while moving his forefinger in a come-here motion inside of her to stimulate her G-spot.

Juice certainly had the juice. His cunnilingus skills were superb, to say the least. His fingers held her thighs in a death-grip as he feasted on her pussy like an escaped prisoner who hadn't had a woman in decades. He licked and sucked her so good that her eyes rolled up in their sockets. Her hips seemed to grow a mind of their own as she began to hump his face so fiercely that soon even his nose was slick with her juices. His tongue proved to be much more pleasurefulthan the sex toy she usually relied on for orgasms.

Her clitoris was sandwiched between his sucking lips, his busy tongue treating it like a speed-bag, when she came. It was a heart-stopping orgasm, so physically intense that her whole body locked up. When Juice kept going, she delivered a series of slaps to the back of his head, and when that didn't work she used every bit of strength she had to pry his mouth away from her defeated nookie.

"Stop, stop, stop, stop, stop," she chanted in an urgent whisper.

Finally, he let go of her thighs. "My bad. I was hungry," he said, lifting himself up on his knees and leaning in between her parted thighs to plant a soft kiss on her chin. "Kush must still be in my system. Feel like I got the munchies."

"That was the best head ever," Bubbles said. "You think so?"

"Oh, yes. Definitely. That took the cake. If that dick is even half as good as that tongue of yours I'm all in."

"Guess I better get to work then, huh?" Juice pushed his boxers down to his knees and back to his feet.

Bubbles had a difficult time keeping her eyes on the TV as

she turned it on, went to an R&B music station, and upped the volume to keep everyone from hearing what was about to go down in her bedroom; her eyes flew from Juice's frighteningly long erection, to the TV, and back tohis erection, watching it bounce up and down like a disturbed diving board as he kicked his boxer shorts to the floor, took two knee-steps back, and slowly pushed the bulbous head into her slippery vaginal opening.

It was a tight fit. He took it easy on her at the start, holding her legs together in one arm, smacking her ass and exploring her breasts with his other hand while long-stroking her cum-slickpussy.

"Grade-A wet-wet," he said, more to himself than anything.

A steady stream of low, whimpering moans escaped her throat, and they became louder ashe quickened the pace of his deep, gut-aching thrusts. His dick was too big. The deeper he drove it in, the more it hurt Bubbles on the inside. But it was a good, welcoming pain. It hurt so good that her eyes watered from the pain of it while at the same time her toes curled from the pleasure.

They both heard his phone when it rang, but neither of them made an attempt to reach for it. The iPhone was face-down on her bedside table. When it stopped ringing it started vibrating. The thought of questioning him about ignoring the call like he did her in the car briefly crossed her mind, but the thought was fleeting and she quickly dismissed it.

A moment later she moved to her hands and knees. Bathed in desolate lamplight, she hugged a pillow and willingly accepted the doggy-style pounding Juice gave her. She lowered her head and the nape of her neck was exposed to him: the long swoop, pale in the lamplight, the gentle slope leading to the base of her skull, the fine spray of hair, the perfect vulnerable arc. He put his hand there on the back of her neck, but his fingers did not close like Bubbles thought they would. Instead, the hand moved downward, between her shoulder blades, down the center of her back, and finally settling on an undulant butt cheek.

"Look at all of this," Juice said, talking to himself again, giving her most of his length with every thrust of his hips.

Bubbles was unable to speak. She could only moan. Her pussy had begun to ache several minutes ago, but it was not an unbearable ache, so she endured it. She could hear him breathing, smell his scent and hers mingling; her nostrils flared like a wolf on the hunt, taking in his smell. The repetitive slap of their bodies coming together was barely audible, but she heard it just as clearly as she heard Juice's breathing, and it was sweeter to her ears than the Usher song that was blaring from her television's surround-sound speaker system.

Twenty minutes passed before she urged him to let her take charge. She got on top of him, reverse cowgirl, and rode his dick for nearly another twenty minutes. She didn't stop until he was completely spent. Falling off to the side of him, she let out a laugh as she waited for her breathing to settle down.

"So," she said, panting, "was it as good as you thought it would be?""No."

Bubbles turned her head so sharply her vertebrae cracked. "What do you mean?" "It was a million times better. No, a billion – a trillion times better."

"Oh." She chuckled. "You came in me.""I know."

"Does this mean you're gonna stop stalking me every time you and your boys come to the club?"

"Nope. Not a chance. I'll be on your ass even more now than I was before. You really done fucked up now."

They shared a laugh. Keeping the smile that the laugh had inspired, Bubbles got up and went to her adjoining bathroom, which could be entered through both walk-in closets. When she came back into the bedroom minutes later she had on a cut-off T-shirt and pink cotton short shorts. Juice had put his boxers back on. She climbed onto his lap and his hands began to roam freely about her derriere.

"Keep it one hundred," he said, "Bulletface bought you this house, didn't he?" "Hell no. I bought this house. He might've contributed a lot of the – "

"In other words, he bought it."

"In other words, don't cut me off. Now, like I was saying, a lot of the money did come from me selling the things he bought me, but he didn't directly buy the place. He doesn't even know where it is. I learned a valuable lesson from his wife last year and that's to never let anyoneknow where you live once you get out of the hood."

"I want you to introduce me to him one day."

Bubbles sucked her teeth indignantly. "Nigga, this ain't Billionaire Matchmaker and I ain't introducing you to no goddamn body."

"You told me how he was getting money with Cup. I want that kind of money. Cup was like my brother. Me and him must've made a million dollars together when we used to hang out on Trumbull every day, but we blew the money as fast as we made it. He's the one who paid for the lawyer that kept me from getting fifty years. I had heard about him flooding the city with dope while I was down. Then he put ten thousand on my books, sent me a bunch of flicks of foreign cars and mansions he owned. I was supposed to ball with him when I got out, just like the old days, but he got killed by that Mexican bitch, who was Blake's wife's sister. That shit went downa month before I was released from Stateville. I got the obituary in the mail the day before Icame home. Didn't even get to see my nigga get buried."

"I remember every day of all that drama," Bubbles said despondently. "I was literally caught right in the middle of all the bullshit. Most of the world looks at Blake's wife and sees this beautiful Texas girl who inherited a huge TV network and billions of dollars from her grandma, but I know who she really is. Alexus Costilla is the real reason I'm so fascinated by that Pablo Escobar show. I know for a fact that she's really a cartel boss just like he was and she'd just as dangerous too. She tried to get me killed – not just once, but several times. That's why I act like my phone's not even ringing when Blake calls. Fuck him and that crazy bitch."

Juice chuckled and his hands slid around from her butt to her thighs as he gazed up at her. She had not yet told him, but she had wanted him ever since she first laid eyes on him. Every physical feature of his had undergone a visual appraisal the moment he'd waved her over for alap dance in the VIP room at Redbone's and Bubbles had come to the conclusion that Juice was one of the finest specimens of man she'd seen in a long time. If he had not been married at the time, she would have made her move right then and there.

"I can understand why you don't fuck with him now," Juice said. He shrugged his broad shoulders. "I got a plug. I'll be good either way. Just figured I could get a better deal than what I got now."

"What's your end goal?""My what?" he asked.

"Your end goal," Bubbles repeated. "Like, is there a certain amount of money you're trying to get before you give it up?"

Juice nodded. "I'm about halfway there."

"Do you plan on settling down with someone and going legit? Once you get to where you want to be cash-wise, I mean."

"I *was* settled down. Then my wife turned into a lesbian."

"She must have a sweet tooth for pussy because no straight

woman in her right mind would leave a nigga who can fuck like you."

Juice's cell rang. He scooped it up and looked at the caller's photo. "It's Dawn. Probably don't want shit." He answered. "What's up, baby girl? What's wrong?"

For the next thirty seconds, he just lay there listening. Bubbles had no idea what was going on, but she knew it was something serious. He tapped her on the thigh, motioning for her to get off his lap, and then he sat up as soon as she did.

"Okay…," he said, "keep me updated." He terminated the call and turned to Bubbles with tears in his eyes.

"Oh, my God, what happened?" she asked.

"They shot Kev," he said. "They shot my nephew."

Chapter 19

On the early morning of Friday, September the ninth, fourteen days after nearly losing his life in the shooting in front of Rev's Barber Shop, Kevin "Kev" Earl emerged from the automatic sliding doors at Northwestern Memorial Hospital in a wheelchair pushed by his wife Tara. A waiting Hummer limo filled with a bunch of his closest family and friends – his and Tara's four children; his sister Rose and her children, including Bankroll Reese; Juice and Bubbles, the new couple that everyone was talking about; and, of course, Suwu, who had saved Kev from certain death – whisked him off to the Villa Taj, his nephew's Burr Ridge mansion, where a bedroom had already been set up for his arrival.

He had suffered two gunshot wounds to his left leg, one in his upper left shoulder, and a fourth round had spiraled through his lower back. It had taken two emergency surgeries to stop the bleeding and to keep him from passing over to the other side.

Juice had been at Kev's bedside for at least a couple of hours every day and when he wasn't there with Kev he was handling business. He'd opened Supreme Hair, Shawnna and Dawn's newhair salon which stood right next to Rev's Barber Shop. He'd sold the house on Central Park Avenue, split the proceeds with his ex-wife, and, with the aid of his attorney, bought a three- story redbrick building on nearby Drake Avenue that had three nice-size apartments and a basement. To match his lady's fly he had gotten himself a white-on-white 2017 BMW 750 Li that put her two-year-old Mercedes to shame. Although he had managed to get all his things moved into the building on Drake Avenue, he had yet to spend even a single night there. Bubbleswasn't having it. She wanted him in bed with her every night, and he wanted the same.

Not long after they'd arrived at the Villa Taj, Kev fell into a Vicodin induced slumber, and Juice left out with Bubbles at his side.

"Where to?" she asked, getting behind the wheel of his silver Jaguar F-Pace SUV.

"Fifteenth and Trumbull," Juice said. "Right up the alley from Redbone's. I need to grab something from a house over there and lay it on Chandra. She'll be waiting on us in the strip club's parking lot."

"Chandra?" Bubbles spit out the word as if she were allergic to it. "You still talk to that… thing?"

"Damn. A *thing*? Why she gotta be a thing?"

"Because she opens her legs for anybody who wants it. And I know about that threesomeyou had with her and Candy. That's so damn gross. Candy's my bitch, but Chandra is beyond trifling. I was so glad when she said you wore protection."

"Hell yeah I wore protection," Juice said. "Every time. Fuck I look like? I know how she get down. Not that I got a problem with it. Hoes make the world go round."

Bubbles rolled her eyes. "I'll slap you and make your head go round."

"You ain't gon' do shit," Juice said, leaning toward her with his lips poised to kiss hercheek.

She leaned away, pressing her shoulder against the driver's door, and pushed his face away. The smug-fitting dark blue mini-dress she had on made her so irresistible to Juice that he moved in for a second kiss, this one proving to be more successful as it crash landed into her rising shoulder. He smiled, flexing his nostrils to inhale her sweet perfume. Apparently, his smile was contagious because Bubbles instantly responded with a smile of her own.

"I don't like you," she said conclusively."Love you more,"

Juice retorted.

"Just make sure you stick to wearing condoms when you're fucking these dirty bitches. I've never tested positive for an STD and I'd really like to keep it that way."

"I usually wear condoms with everybody."

"Everybody?" Another repeated word she was seemingly allergic to. "How many bitches areyou fucking?"

"That depends on how many different personalities you got," he said.

"I'm serious, Juice. Please let me know if it's more than just me. I'll put up with a lot, but I'm not risking my life for anybody. I'd rather go another fourteen months without sex than to deal with a nigga I have to share with a whole 'nother bitch."

"I haven't fucked anybody since we got together.""Put it on Cup's grave."

"It ain't that serious. If I say I ain't fucked nobody else, that's what it is. Fuck I gotta lie for?"

"I'm just making sure." Bubbles went silent for all of ten seconds. "You know what? From now on, we're using protection. Fuck the bullshit. You are not about to have me up in somebody's clinic looking like somebody's thot. Ms. Linda ain't raise no fools."

With a silent chuckle, Juice went to the Chicago Sun-Times app he'd downloaded to his iPhone and checked out the top stories. With election day drawing near, there were dozens of Trump versus Clinton articles. The Mayor was making plans to add a thousand new cops to the CPD in a desperate measure to combat the city's surge in gun violence. There had already been more than five hundred homicides in Chicago this year – more than Los Angeles and New York City combined. The ongoing gang wars in the North Lawndale neighborhood accounted for forty-nine of this year's gun deaths, including four murders Juice had ordered in the days following the shooting that had hospitalized Kev. So far this year, North Lawndale was second to only Englewood in regards to murder rate increases.

As Bubble was hanging a left on Roosevelt Road, getting ready to enter North Lawndale via Kedzie Avenue, Juice pulled a .45-caliber Glock from his loose-fitting jeans and racked the slide, chambering a hollow-tipped round. He set the semiautomatic on his lap and kept his finger on the trigger as he began studying the faces of every driver and pedestrian in sight. Bubbles became just as vigilant.

"I hate driving through here," she said. "All I can think about is what happened to Kev and Lil Dave… and Junior. That's why I moved out of the hood. I know we all gotta go one day, but let me get some gray hairs first. I love my life. Fuck the bullshit."

Juice could do nothing but shake his head. Growing up on Trumbull Avenue, he had always been tangled up in gang-related beefs, usually over turf, but for the most part he and Cup had been more about making money. They had resorted to violence only when it was absolutely necessary. Nowadays, the younger generation had it all backwards. They were all about shooting and banging so much so that making money often came second on their itineraries, if it came at all. Juice knew that, no matter how deeply entwined he had to be in the gang warfare, he would never lose the desire to make money the tax-free way. The truth of the matter was that that Juice was and always would be in love with the dope game.

Which was why he was meeting up with his old side-chick in the parking lot of a seedy strip club. Chandra's frequent bouts of promiscuity had led her to the bed of the Bowlegs, the leader of a clique of south side Gangsta Disciples. Bowlegs had a huge swath of territory under his control in West Englewood, according to what Chandra had told Juice, but the guy Bowlegs was buying his cocaine from was charging him close to forty thousand dollars per kilo. To make matters worse, the cocaine Bowlegs was getting from the supplier was oil-based, which made it more difficult to cook up and step on. Juice had fish-scale bricks of cocaine, the best dope in the city. His Mexican supplier, Hector Ortega, got the kilos straight from Mexico and he only charged Juice nineteen thousand for each kilogram. So, Juice had offered Bowlegs a kilo for thirty thousand. That had been last week. Apparently satisfied with the first deal, Bowlegs was back for more. This time he was looking to buy three kilos.

Juice instructed Bubbles to pull over into the grass-less backyard at 1530 South Trumbull Avenue next to a red Chevy Suburban. He dug a cheap Virgin Mobile flip phone out of a front pocket and dialed a number.

"Whose house is this?" Bubbles asked.

Revealing the blueprint of his drug operation to a woman he barely knew --or to anyone for that matter -- was never going to happen. He couldn't risk telling her that the house they were parked behind was headquarters for the Traveler Vice Lords; that its basement was stocked with inventory of forty-one assault rifles, sixty-eight sub-machine guns, twelve shotguns, and nearly two hundred handguns; that at all times there were at least ten gang members in the house, ready to carry out any order given to them by Juice, usually through Kev. And Juice certainly couldn't tell her that the house across the street from TVL headquarters was one of his drug houses where he currently had seven brick-shaped kilos of cocaine and twenty-eight pounds of high-grade marijuana stashed in a deep freezer.

Wayno, the dread-headed twenty-year-old who was taking Kev's place for the moment as Juice's second in command, answered the phone.

"I'm out here in the back," Juice said. "Run across the street and grab me three o them snowcones. Send me some S out here too."

"I'm on it," Wayno said.

Juice flipped the phone shut. Bubbles was staring at him. "What?" he asked.

"Don't act like you didn't hear me. Whose house is this?"

"It's one of Rell's properties, the nigga Tamera got married to last year.""I'm not talking about who *owns* it. I wanna know who lives here."

"Ah. I see what you mean." Juice grinned."Well?" Bubbles asked.

"I plead the fifth."

"If you got me involved with anything illegal I'm getting out of this truck and calling an Uber to take me home. This is not *Mob Wives*. I didn't sign up for this. It should be my choice ifI want to get in on your bullshit."

"Is bullshit your favorite curse word?"

"No, I just say it around you a lot because you're always so full of it. Now let me know whatthe hell kind of bullshit you got me in."

Juice chuckled but said nothing. He knew what would get Bubbles off his case and he wasalready searching for it on his iPhone. He found it and showed it to her.

"These are so beautiful," she said, her eyes widening as she looked at the photo.

It was a screenshot of a pair of striped Salvatore Ferragamo boots that Juice had run acrosswhile online shopping two mornings ago.

"You getting a pair of these for me?" she asked.

"If you can shut up and let me handle my business."

"Okay, I'll shut up." She put an imaginary key to her lips

and turned it. Her sexy wise-ass grin surfaced. She handed over his iPhone and started doing something on hers.

Seconds later, five dread-headed Vice Lords-- two of them carrying AK-47 assault riffles-- poured out of the back door of TVL headquarters and loaded into the red Suburban. Then,Wayno came jogging down the stairs with a brown paper grocery bag in one hand and a Glock inthe other. He stopped at Juice's window.

"Lay that on Chandra," Juice said, "and get the money from her. If it's not ninety bands don't take it. She'll be in a blue Jeep behind Redbone's."

"Same as last time," Wayno said, nodding.

"Yeah, same Jeep," Juice confirmed. "Make her get in the Suburban with you this time, put the ball in our court. Bring the bread to the salon. Baby gotta get her nails done."

"A'ight. I got some info for you about that nigga Darren, too. I'll chop it up with you at the salon." Wayno walked away and got behind the wheel of the Suburban.

Juice had seen Bubble glance his way when he'd said 'ninety bans' and he knew she was just itching to ask him about it, but the imaginary mouth-lock remained in place. He told her to follow the Suburban out of the alley. She started the F-Pace's powerful engine and obeyed his order while he sent Chandra a text message from the flip phone telling her to bring the cash tothe red Suburban.

They rode past the strip club's parking lot and onto 16th Street and Bubbles broke her silence as she made a u-turn to park in front of Juice's BMW, which Shawnna and Dawn had driven to work every day this week.

"Can I talk now?" she asked. "It's not about your business, I swear. It's about the guys you all are beefing with."

Juice didn't say anything. From where they were parked he could see a narrow portion of thcparking lot behind Redbone's.

He saw the blue Jeep and the front end of the Suburban.

"Okay, I'll take that as a yes," Bubbles said. "The boy who shot Kev is paralyzed now, right?"

"Yeah. Keep your eyes on the street before I end up being the next nigga in a wheelchair."

Looking around she said, "If Big Jay is paralyzed I think he should get a pass. I mean, isn't that punishment enough?"

"It's not up to me if he gets it. The only nigga I'm after is the one who killed my son. If Kev wants Big Jay dead, then that's what it'll be."

"Do you think something bad happened to Kobe? He's been missing for two whole weeks. Tamia said she still hasn't heard from him since she heard him getting into a scuffle or something the day Kev got shot."

"Ain't no telling what happened to that dude. Knowing him, he's probably somewhere laid up with another chick. I personally don't care where he's at. Ain't thought about him since Shawnna broke up with him."

Of course Juice was lying. Kobe's charred and dismembered remains were in two trash bagsin the trunk of his Chevy Caprice, which sat in his elderly grandmother's garage in South Lawndale. Juice had paid Wayno a thousand dollars to drive it there a couple of hours after Kev was shot.

He breathed a sigh of relief as the Suburban cruised out of the alley and turned towards him, while the Jeep took the parking lot's front entrance and headed off in the other direction. He put the Glock on his waist, covering it with his black T-shirt, and opened his door. Clad in Louis Vuitton from neck to toe with a gold Rolex Oyster Perpetual Datejust 41 watch on his wrist and athick gold Cuban-link chain draped around his neck, he stepped out of his Jaguar SUV (covered with Rhodium silver paint with 28-inch Forgiato rims) looking like the king he felt God hadmade him to be. He waited for Bubbles to join him on the sidewalk. She'd gotten her hair dyed blond and whipped into a neat bob there at the salon a few days ago and it made her look even more beautiful than before. Juice gave her a sharp smack on the ass and a peck on the cheek when she made it to his side. Then, he let her lead the way into Supreme Hair.

With it being a Friday, Juice wasn't surprised to find the hair salon packed with women getting their hair and nails done for whatever weekend celebrations they planned to attend. But, what did surprise him was how they all got quiet when he walked in. Then, he saw what his daughter Shawnna had in her hand and he understood the silence.

Chapter 20

"What the fuck are you doing holding a pregnancy test?" Juice asked coldly.

Shawnna's eyes dropped faster than Humpty-Dumpty when he fell from that wall. She cast a wide-eyed stare at the diamond-shaped black tiles with gold inlays trying to figure out not only how this had happened but also how she was going to explain it to her father.

"Lord Jesus," someone murmured.

Not wanting to get embarrassed any more than she already had in front of everyone in the shop, Shawnna turned and headed into her office. Just thirty minutes earlier she had complained to Dawn about the fogged glass on their office doors and windows; now she was grateful for the privacy. She sunk down into the black leather swivel behind her desk and awaited the inevitable, holding the test between her thumb and forefinger while shaking her head in disbelief.

Juice stormed in and slammed the door shut. He crossed his arms over his powerfully-built chest and, like a true Chicago bull, blew a heavy breath of air from his flared nostrils.

"I'm just as shocked as you are," Shawnna said, beginning her defense. "I haven't the slightest idea how this could've happened. Reese and I haven't been having unprotected sex and you know he's the only guy I've been with since Kobe."

Juice shut his eyes and shook his head. He lifted his hands to his face and shook his head again. "I though we had an agreement on this. Do you remember the agreement? No babies until marriage."

Tears of disappointment began to sprout forth from Shawnna's eyes just as Juice lowered his hands from over his face revealing a grin as wide as the Grinch's and effectively confusing the hell out of Shawnna.

"You honestly believed I was mad?" He laughed, walked around the desk, and gave her a hug. "Baby girl, I love you no matter what. Never thought I'd be a granddaddy before I hit thirty,but I'm not complaining about it."

"So you're not mad?" Shawnna asked, full-on sobbing now."I don't have the right to be mad. You're a grown woman."

She picked a tissue from the box of Kleenex on her glass-topped desk and dabbed the streaks of tears from her face. "I'm disappointed in myself. You know how young and wild Reese is. He's not gonna want a baby. Hell, *I* don't even want a baby. That's why I always use protection and when I say always, I literally mean that. Not one time have we done anything without a condom. I cannot for the life of me understand how this could've happened."

Juice rubbed a hand up and down her shoulders and kissed her on the temple. His lips stayed there for a moment. The warm embrace settled her nerves and by the time he pulled back she hadstopped crying.

The office door swung open and Dawn walked in slowly. She had her head down and her eyes up, like a dog approaching her master after having left a pile of poop on the kitchen floor. "Daddy," Dawn said, "don't be mad with her. If anything the blame should be placed on--"

"I'm not mad," Juice said, heading back around the desk. "Let me talk to Wayno right quick." And just like that he was gone.

Dawn tried to leave out behind him.

"Nuh-uh, bitch," Shawnna said. "Turn right back around, close that door, look me square in the eyes, and tell me exactly what the fuck you was about to tell Daddy."

Dawn, dressed identical to Shawnna in a tight black dress and heels, stopped dead in her tracks, dropped her head back, and let out a loud sigh. Reluctantly, she kicked the door shut and spun to face her sister.

"Talk," Shawnna said, squinting.

Dawn hesitated. "Okay, here it is," she said finally. "Remember that day we went on the date with Reese and Luke? When they took us shopping and out to dinner at that nice soul food restaurant?"

"Remember the last time I punched you in the face?" "Don't threaten me."

"Don't play with me," Shawnna replied.

Following another hesitant moment, Dawn said, "I might have accidentally poked a hole in that condom you had in your purse when you and Reese fucked in his car at the Villa Taj right before they took us shopping."

Shawnna's squint tightened as searched her brain for the details of that day. It was the day

their brother was murdered, the day their mother left their father for a woman, but the memory pushing its way to the forefront of Shawnna's mind had nothing to do with either of those heartbreaking events. No, it was the memory of what had happened in the elevator that took them from the Villa Taj's foyer to its massive underground parking garage that was playing in high- definition on the big scree of her mind's eye. Before they'd stepped off of the elevator Dawn had suddenly realized that their identical purses had *somehow* gotten mixed up during a trip they tookto a beauty supply store.

"You dirty bitch!" Shawnna said, emphasizing each word and looking down at the pregnancy test with a new level of understanding. "You took my bag…poked holes in my condoms…and then gave the bag back to me, pretending to have accidentally grabbed the wrong one. And you even had the nerve to remind me to use protection when I got in the car with him."

"I know." Dawn flopped down in the chair on the opposite side of the desk from Shawnna. "I'm a horrible sister."

"So," Shawnna said, looking up, "the whole time I've been throwing up this week you knew I was pregnant? And you didn't even fucking tell me?"

"I didn't know *how* to tell you. I mean, you *are* the evil twin, remember? And nobody likes getting punched in the face."

Instinctively, Shawnna launched the pregnancy test at Dawn's face. Dawn ducked, but the plastic stick still whacked her on the forehead.

"Ouch!" Dawn frowned and rubbed her forehead. "See? See what I mean? Ain't nobody got time for that."

"Why would you do some stupid shit like that?"

"I don't know. I guess I was taking what Myesha told us about how to trap a rich nigga to heart. I didn't want Reese just using you like he does every other bitch he sees with a cute face and a nice body and I definitely didn't want you going back to that broke ass Kobe if shit didn't work out with you and Reese. Plus, we need somebody to hold us down if Daddy ever has to go back to prison. With the kind of money Reese has, those child support checks will be fat."

"Reese and I are not breaking up anytime soon," Shawnna said, though she honestly believed that Reese was already cheating and that a break-up was on the horizon. "I understand you were trying to look out for the both of us--in your own sick, twisted way--but you should have let me make that decision."

"I'm sorry, Sister. I really am. I made a big mistake and I'm really, truly sorry about it."

"Are you really?" Shawnna asked, cocking her head to the side.

Dawn nodded rapidly, indicating that she was indeed sorry about what she'd done, but her burgeoning grin said otherwise. "So, are you keeping it?"

"What kind of question is that? Of course I'm keeping it. I'm not about to kill my child.""But what if Reese doesn't want it?"

"Then Reese doesn't want me."

"Yes!" Dawn threw her fists in the air. "I'm gonna be an aunt!""Really, Dawn?"

"Yes, really. Now all we gotta do is get Daddy to pop one in Bubbles so we can have two babies running around the house."

"If you think Daddy's about to have another baby you're just as crazy as Mama."

"Girl, please," Dawn said, standing up. "You see how thick and pretty that girl is? Her buttis like yours and mine put together. And you know she's probably doing all those stripper movesin the bedroom. No way he's pulling outta that."

Shawnna stood, squinting again, and shook her head. "I don't know what makes peoplethink you're the good one," she said.

"It's simple." Dawn walked to the door and pulled it open. "I'm the lesser of two evils." Sheleft out and shut the door behind her.

Chapter 21

"Are you ever gonna turn off that stupid game?"

Darren smiled at Amanda, the big-breasted, blue-eyed white girl he'd met a few hours after rushing Big Jay to the hospital two weeks ago. He had left the Camaro at a relative's house and hailed a cab that took him downtown where he'd checked into a room at the Trump before heading back out for a drink. A half hour later he had found himself standing outside under the lighted sign of Old Times Sake, a bar and restaurant four blocks east of the Trump. Amanda had asked him for a light.

"What kind of bar doesn't let you smoke?" she'd asked, sparking the conversation that led to her inviting him into her ramshackle Orland Park apartment, which was where he was now; sitting on the cushy sofa in her small, cluttered living room with his left eye squinted against the smoke rising from the cigarette in the corner of his mouth.

His smile lasted less than five seconds. He paused the game, ashed his cigarette, and gave Amanda the attention she sought.

She was thirty-three, according to what she'd told him, but her driver's license put her date of birth at October 8, 1979, which meant she was actually a month away from thirty-seven. It also meant that she was by far the oldest woman he'd ever been sexually involved with. Per his request, she wore nothing but a Cubs t-shirt that stopped just above her pale knee caps. Her long hair was pulled back in a ponytail. An inch of makeup coated her face, thoroughly concealing the crow's feet on the outside of her eyes and the lines on her wide forehead.

Darren was nobody's fool--never had been, never would be. He knew why she wanted his attention. Late last night he had cleared off the table in her kitchen and emptied his suitcase full of cash onto it. He took a picture of the tall pile of cash--more that $120,000.00 in total--and posted it on his Instagram page with the caption 'Turn up 2nite at Club Stadium, who comin' throo?'. He'd stuffed the cash back into the suitcase and returned it to the trunk of his Camaro, which he had just gotten back after paying close to seventeen hundred dollars for the removal of all the blood Big Jay had left on the interior. Amanda had been clinging to him ever since. He'd been treated to breakfast in bed earlier this morning followed by a back massage and the best blowjob she'd given him thus far. She'd washed and dried his clothes, rolled up four fat joints for him, and sucked him off again an hour ago. Now, she was standing off to the side of him lighting the last joint with her red Bic lighter.

He put down the Xbox One controller and looked up at her. "You just want some attention,"he said.

"I want"--she coughed from the potent weed smoke-- "a hell of a lot more than some attention." She passed him the joint, coughed thrice, and then put her hands on her hips. "What did you do, rob a bank or something? How'd you get all that money?"

Darren took a long drag from the joint. "You got me smoking like a white boy. I'm a street nigga. We smoke blunts. Not joints, not weed pipes, not water bongs. Just cigarillo wraps and cigar wraps. Brown blunts."

"I don't care about any of that," Amanda said.

"Of course you don't," Darren countered. "Just like every woman I know, all you care aboutis dick and money. And not necessarily in that order."

"Everybody needs money.""I know that's right."

"Come on, Roger. Spit it out. Where'd you get the cash?"

"It's a card scam," he said, eyeing the burning end of the joint and blowing smoke out of his nose as he manufactured yet another lie. “See, I started off with fifty bucks. My cousin Tamia works at a Chase bank on the south side. She told me she could give me back ten times the amount of whatever I give her. Something about being able to add a zero on the computer and all I had to do was give her ten percent when I got the money. Long story short, I gave her fifty before she went to work and when she came home she handed me a bank card with five hundred on it. The next time it was four hundred for four thousand, then twenty-five hundred for twenty- five thousand, and now that’s what we do once a week, the twenty-five.”

“And that works every time?”“Every time.”

“Twenty-five grand?”

“Every single week,” he said, nodding his head in the affirmative as he passed her the joint. “I ain’t did it in the past two weeks, but that’s only because I got so much cash saved up.”

“You don’t worry about going to jail?”

“Nah. If anybody goes down it’ll be her. It’s not like I work at the bank, you feel me?”“Whose names are the cards in?”

“Mine. It’s just one car. I take the money off and give it back.”“At an ATM?”

“Yeah. A bunch of ATMs. You know they got limits sometimes. Not on the card, though.

No limit on the card. You can get as much as the ATM will let you get until the card is empty.” “You’re shitting me. Hmmmm.” She nodded thoughtfully.

They were halfway through the joint when she said, “I’ve got about three thousand dollars in my savings account. Think you can get your cousin to help me out? I’d greatly appreciate it.”

“Yeah, I can do that.” He put on another incredibly brief smile. “You gotta do somethingfor me too, though.”

"Something like what?"

"I don't know. Something." Darren shrugged. "Just tell me," she insisted.

"Go and get the money. We'll talk about what I want when you get back. That way I'll have time to think about it."

Amanda didn't wait to finish the joint. She slipped on a pair of jeans and sandals, went to the bathroom, and got the keys to her Honda CR-V before rushing out of the door.

While she was gone, Darren packed up his things--his Xbox One and its many accessories, a couple of outfits, and some hygiene items--and took it all outside to his Camaro where he stuffed it all in the trunk with his suitcase. Then, he got behind the wheel, pulled out his smartphone, and checked his Instagram page.

Just as he expected, the photo he'd uploaded last night had received a ton of attention from many of his followers. The photo had 972 likes and 81 comments. Most of the comments were from people he'd gone to school with or knew from his neighborhood, but there was one comment from a sexy light-skinned girl he'd met on Facebook; an "Instagram Model" named Kaira who had over a hundred thousand followers. Her comment was nothing more than a two- eyed emoji, but it was enough to excite Darren.

He direct messaged her: *You should come to the club with me tonight.*

It took her only half a minute to respond: *Hml 773-555-2212*

Darren's eyes lit up. He couldn't believe she'd given up her phone number so easily. He dialed the number and was just about to hit the call key when the unmistakable rumble of Amanda's CR-V compelled him to stop what he was doing. He saved the number to his contacts and looked up just as Amanda was pulling into the parking space to the right of his car. She got out of the CR-V and got in next to him, handing him a cash-filled envelope. He put the envelope on the dashboard and started the engine.

"You talk to your cousin?" she asked, clicking her seat belt into place.

"Yeah, she said come on up to the bank. She can do it while we're there. Don't tell nobody Idid this for you either. I mean *nobody.*"

"I won't say a word." "I'm serious, Amanda."

"I promise you I won't say a word to *anyone* about how I got the money. I'll say I won it at the casino."

"I don't care if you say you found it in the middle of the road. Just keep me and my cousin out of it." He moved his seat back a notch, thumbed his gym shorts and boxer briefs down to his knees, and glanced over at Amanda as he drove out of the parking lot.

In the two weeks since their fling had begun Amanda had yet to hesitate to get busy when hepulled out what she liked to call his "BBC", but this time was different; she had more questions.

"There's twenty-nine hundred and forty bucks in that envelope," she said with a forefinger pointed at the envelope. "Will she do all of that?"

"Yeah. You'll get twenty-nine thousand and four hundred, minus ten percent." "Okay, that's twenty-six thousand four hundred and sixty."

"I don't know what it is. I didn't add the shit up." Darren was getting frustrated. He wanted his dick sucked. He curled his fingers around its base and shook it.

"I'm just trying to get our business squared away first," she said, not even glancing at his shaking penis. "This is going to be so big for me. You don't even understand. I'm getting out of that piece of shit apartment as soon as my lease is up in December. Wait until John gets a load ofthis. He'll shit bricks for a hundred weeks. And you know what? Him and Jessica can kiss the whole shitty circle of my asshole."

Frowning, Darren pulled his underwear and shorts back up. "Who in the fuck is John?" he asked.

"John's my ex-husband. The no-good son of a bitch ran off with my sister, Jessica, a year and a half ago…cleared out my accounts and skipped town. He stole twelve thousand dollars from me, twelve grand of my hard-earned, goddamn money! The two rotten fuckers are living in a trailer park somewhere in Kentucky. I'll tell you what, when I get this money I'm gonna get mea new car just so I can drive down there and take a shit on their front porch. Mark my words, Roger. You watch and see."

Darren's frown deepened. "I don't wanna see that shit." He turned in to a BP gas station andeased to a stop at pump three. He handed Amanda two twenties. "Put twenty on pump three and grab me a pack of Newport 100s."

"Mind if I get a pack of Marlboro reds for myself?" Amanda asked. "I'll pay you back once we leave the bank."

"Go ahead."

"Thanks, Roger. You're a life saver." She pecked him on the jaw as he put the Camaro in park and then they opened their doors at the same time.

Amanda took off on a fast-paced walk to the front door of the gas station, past a heavyset white man pumping gas into a Dodge pickup. The fat guy looked at her ass until she disappearedinto the gas station.

Darren shut his door and sped off, shaking his head at the crazy white woman as he drove away with $2,940.00 of her hard-earned goddamn money.

Chapter 22

They had left the North Lawndale area far behind and were now entering Lake Forest. Bubbles took a turn to the left and then drove perhaps a half a mile into an area of increasingly large and luxurious houses. The Jaguar navigated a long, snaking road that rose toward the crest of a hill. A half a mile along she made a right onto one of a number of sweeping streets of large Colonial houses with slate roofs, formal English gardens, and impeccably manicured lawns. Finally, she pulled into her driveway, stopped on the concrete apron directly in front of the garage doors, and got out. To one side of the the leftmost door was a small steel box. Swinging up the protective panel, she punched in a number on the keypad and one of the garage doors opened. She got back behind the wheel, drove the Jaguar into the garage, and then shut the door. Next to them was her Mercedes.

"I love this house," she said, leading him inside.

"Yeah, the house is nice and the neighborhood looks good, but all the people are old, white, and racist. It ain't safe for niggas like us."

"Whatever, Lee. This neighborhood is patrolled by members of a private security firm. Allthe men are ex-cops and half of them are black. They know every face in the neighborhood."

Juice was astonished. "You can't seriously believe that none of your neighbors are racist."

She heard the disbelieving edge to his voice. "It doesn't matter to me whether they're racist or not. The fact that they carry themselves like civilized human beings is what makes me want toraise my daughter here. I'm more worried about a black man putting a bullet in me or my baby's head than a racist white man doing it. Especially in Chicago. The whole point of getting money is supposed to be to make a better situation for yourself and your family, am I right? It shouldn't be about buying more guns to kill people. That's dumb. Period."

In the spacious living room, Juice threw himself across the sofa and got comfortable. He decided it was best to shut his mouth and turn to ESPN. Otherwise, he was digging himself into an argument he couldn't win.

"Are you hungry?" Bubbles asked from the kitchen "Nah, I'm good. Just bring me a beer."

"I'm…uh…planning something nice for us this weekend."
"It's the weekend now."

"I know that. But it's still early in the day. What I'm talking about"--she crossed the threshold into the living room carrying a bottle of Budweiser for him and an Evian water for herself-- "doesn't start until later tonight and it'll last until early Monday morning. Are you free all weekend?"

He cracked open the beer and sat up thinking. Was he free all weekend? Of course he wasn't. Wayno had just told him that some girl had called asking about the $50,000.00 hit on Darren and saying that she knew where he was going to be later on tonight. There was no way Juice was going anywhere until his son's killer was captured or killed.

Bubbles was standing with her left side facing him and her eyes on her iPhone. Juice looked up and stared at the perfect spherical roundness of her huge butt and immediately experienced a change of heart. Suddenly, being present for Darren's last breaths didn't seem so important. His eyes traveled down her thick legs to the Miu Miu pumps on her feet and then shot back up to the massive hump of her ass. She'd gotten her fingernails painted the same shade of blue that her dress was and her lipstick was a shade or two lighter.

"Big Booty Bubbles wears blue," he said and cracked up laughing. "If I ever write a book about our relationship, that's what I'm naming it."

"Can I continue with my weekend plans or not?" "What kind of plans?"

"It involves a plane and a boat."

"A plane and a boat," Juice repeated, taking a sip of his beer. "I don't know if I can rockwith that. Sounds like white folks' activities to me."

"You're the only real racist person in this neighborhood." "*I'm* racist? How can I possibly be racist? All I sell is white." Bubbles smirked. "Drugs don't count."

"Where is this plane and boat supposed to be taking us?"

"To south Florida, a small town about fifty miles north of Miami. My mom's sister Gabby isdown there." She turned to him, eyes wide. "Aunt Gabby's boyfriend is taking her gator fishing! Can you believe it?"

"What the fuck is gator fishing?"

"You throw out a line with some bait on it, wait for an alligator to bite, then you shoot it and pull it onto the boat. Should be a piece of cake." She said it like it was the most normal activity in the world.

Juice wasn't having it. "Are you out of your fucking mind? Gator fishing? Nigga! *Hell*, no. Hell no *again*! I see these white people must really be rubbing off on you. You're officially one of them."

She laughed. "No, I'm not. I'm just…adventurous. A risk-taker.""You can take that risk by yourself."

"You're no fun."

"Look, you got the wrong kinda nigga right here. I'm not sky-diving, bungee jumping, swimming with sharks or none of that kinda shit and I sure in the fuck ain't about to do no gator fishing."

Bubbles pouted, regarding Juice with a silent stare. Then, slowly, the pout lifted into a smile."I was just playing. About the gator fishing, not the plane and the boat. My girl Tasia wants us tofly down to Miami and join her and her new fiance on his yacht for a nice little couples weekend getaway. She got engaged to some big real estate tycoon a couple of months ago. They're inviting nine couples. Everybody else is either engaged or married, but she really wants us to come too. Me and her are both in our first relationships since Blake."

"Wait, he was fucking you and her?""It's complicated, but yes."

"You can cancel those plans," Juice said, shaking his head. "I'm not going to your THOT reunion."

Bubbles rolled her eyes. She sat down next to him, firing off text messages and Facebook updates on her smartphone while he watched *SportsCenter*, drank his beer, and replied to a fewof his own text messages. There were only three of them: Chandra wanted a thousand dollars for her role in the multi-kilo deal with Bowlegs; his mom, Sheryl, needed to borrow five hundred dollars to pay for a new set of car tires; his sister, Malaysia, who lived with a boyfriend and five kids in Nashville, needed a loan for the same amount his mom wanted, which meant his mom didn't really need new tires. He sent the same reply to all three messages: *Okay, will send in a couple of hours.*

He placed his phone on the arm of the sofa and sank deeper into the soft leather. The living room was his favorite room in this large house. There was a polished wood floor, devoid of any carpets, the tan leather sofa and two matching chairs, a glass coffee table with curved bronze legs, and an over-sized stone fireplace on might expect to find in a hunting lodge. Against one wall was an antique walnut China cabinet, displaying plates and bowls behind diamond panes of glass. On the other wall there was a large painting--a portrait in dark, brooding hues of a seated Michelle Obama, young and arresting, her hands held loosely in her lap, her heard thrown back almost in defiance, large eyes regarding the viewer with a peculiar intensity; there was something about her intent of motion as if she were an arrow in a drawn bow about to catapult across the room.

"Who painted--"

"Don't talk to me right now," Bubbles said sharply, decapitating Juice's question before he could even get it all the way out. "I'm not in the mood to talk to somebody who rains plans for a living."

Juice laughed heartily. "You mad at me?"

"Laugh all you want. We'll see who's laughing tonight." "What's that supposed to mean?"

"It means if I'm not on a flight to some kind of romantic weekend getaway by the end of thenight, your new nickname is gonna be No Juice. I had to pay a good amount of money for this dress and I'll be damned if I don't get to have a good time in it. Ra'Mya's staying the weekend ather auntie Shay's house. This will be my only free weekend for a long while. I'm not about to letyou fuck me out of it."

"Nah, I won't fuck you out of it." He finished off the beer, dropped the depleted bottle into a short trash can that stood beside the sofa, and turned to her, his expression cheerful and amused. "But I'll fuck you into it." He grabbed her by both shoulders and pushed her onto her back.

"Get the fuck off me," she said, but she did nothing to stop his hands from pushing up her dress or his tongue from penetrating the sweet glistening folds of her pussy.

Chapter 23

Bankroll Reese's remedy for anger (and also depression, pain, unhappiness, boredom, et cetera) was lean--tall ice-filled Styrofoam cups of the narcotic beverage. He drank enough Actavis Prometh with Codeine syrup to be crowned an honorary spokesperson for Actavis. Add a few blunts of Kush and a Xanax pill to the mix and he wouldn't know the meaning of a worry.

His rose gold Rolex read 11:59 A.M. He had taken two Xanax bars before he lit up his first blunt and poured up his first cup of Lean. Now, as he sat in the backseat of his blacked-out Rolls Royce Phantom (not the convertible Drophead Coupe, which sat in his driveway at the Burr Ridge estate, but the hard-top sedan) hidden behind the black curtains that covered its rear windows, he lit another blunt and sucked in a mouthful of smoke. He inhaled deeply and held it in. He wanted to be as high as he could get when he walked into The Visionary Lounge.

The nightclub, located on the corner of Laramie and Chicago Avenue on the Windy City's west side, had been closed ever since Reese's father was gunned down inside of it late last year. It had undergone a two-million dollar renovation since then and was slated to reopen at nine o'clock tonight.

For the first time since his father's funeral, Bankroll Reese wore a suit--a pitch-black Ermenegildo Zegna with black leather Christian Louboutin loafers. His bloodshot eyes were tucked behind sunglasses--a pair of Louis Vuittons that had belonged to Cup.

It was the Lean that kept him from crying.

Dialing his girlfriend's number on his iPhone, he took another sip of the Sprite and purple Actavis mix. They went to FaceTime video chat and he saw that she was wiping tears from her beautiful face.

"Let me guess," she said, sniffling, "one of them bitches at the shop done sent you a text or some shit. Ugh, I can't stand nosy bitches."

"Baby, what are you talking about? Ain't nobody sent me no texts."

She paused and wiped her face again. In the background he could see a girl moving about at a stove, but he didn't recognize the kitchen.

"I really don't think I should tell you over the phone," Shawnna said.

"Tell me," Reese told her. He put the Styrofoam in the cup holder next to his seat. "You know I don't do surprises. And where you at? Whose house is that? Who is that standing behind you at the stove?"

"That's Myesha. I'm at her house."

"Hey Reese," Myesha said without looking back. "Tell me what the fuck is going on," Reese demanded.

"Okay, okay." Shawnna sniffled. "So I came into the shop this morning and headed straight into my office with Dawn. We had to talk over some new hires and some other hair stuff. We hadn't been in the office a good five minutes when I grabbed the trashcan and puked up my breakfast. With that being the fourth time I've thrown up this week--"

"Fourth time?" Reese frowned.

"Yeah," she said. "Twice when we were moving into the new place on Drake, once last night, and the fourth time at the shop this morning."

"Why am I just now hearing about this?"

"Because I didn't think anything of it at first. Not until this morning. When it happened this time Dawn was like, 'you might wanna go to a doctor and see if there's a baby in there somewhere'. So, I went to the corner store and bought a pregnancy test."

"And?"

"It was positive."

"So you're pregnant?"

"Apparently so. I just took three other pregnancy tests to be absolutely sure. All of themgave the same result."

Reese's mouth fell open and his brows lifted in surprise. Then, his lips came together and rose into a small grin. The thin-lipped grin grew wider as he imagined himself clutching a tiny little body to his chest, a child that he had helped to create. He'd been thinking about having akid ever since last year when he'd inherited his father's fortune. He wanted to do the same thing one day and there was no woman better to do it with than Shawnna Wilkins.

"I'll take it you're not so thrilled about this news," she said.

"No, I am. I'm definitely happy. I'm just too high to express it right now." He chuckled onceand took a nice long pull on the blunt. "This gotta be some kind of message from my pops. It can't be a coincidence that the same day I'm reopening The Visionary Lounge to the public I find out my girl's pregnant. He had a hand in this. Can't nobody tell me different."

"Aren't you wondering how this could happen when we use protection all the time?"Shawnna asked.

"Hell no. That's the last thing on my mind. I'm just glad I don't have to wear that shit no more." His grin stretched wider.

"You would say that." She rolled her eyes. Myesha said, "Congrats, Reese."

"Will you tell your friend to mind her goddamn business back there?""No, I won't." Shawnna laughed.

"You need to." He hit the blunt. "You told Juice yet?"

"He walked in on me when I was telling the girls in the

shop about it. I thought he'd be pissed but he's actually excited about it."

"For real? Damn. That's what's up. So, you're gon' move in with me now, right? At leastuntil you have the baby. I don't want you over there on Drake with my baby in your stomach."

"I'll move in with you when you get your mind right and put a ring on it.""Put a ring on it?"

"Did I stutter? Yes, put a ring on it.""Where did this idea come from?" "The Bible."

Reese shook his head, grinning broadly. "You gon' be my date to the club tonight or what?

You know I gotta show up with some eye candy."

"Show up with another bitch if you want to," Shawnna warned. "Pregnant or not, I'll stomp a mud-hole in a bitch. Now try me."

"Damn, where that come from? I asked you to be my date."

"I'm just saying. You talking about some damn *eye candy*. I better be the *only* eye candy.""You coming with me or not?"

"Yes, I'm coming. I'm about to eat in a few minutes, then I'll go home and find me something to wear while I wait for Myesha to get back from her one o'clock dentist appointment."

"She need to get her teeth glued together," Reese said. "Bye, boy." Rolling her eyes, Shawnna ended the call.

Reese looked up and smiled. He was still smiling when Chubb, his driver, pulled to a stop at the curb in front of the five-story yellow-brick building that was The Visionary Lounge.

As usual there was a bunch of traffic on Chicago Avenue and since Reese had long ago become somewhat of a celebrity to many west-siders, he was unmoved by the elated shouts he heard as he stepped out of the Rolls Royce, still smoking his blunt and sipping from his cup. He strode purposefully into the nightclub, followed closely by Chubb and Suwu, who also wore black suits and ties for this special occasion.

Standing in two long lines along the front of the bar were the nightclub's fifty person staff of employees--bartenders, waitresses, chefs, bottle girls, a ten-man security team, and Kathy, the no-nonsense, forty-year-old Reese had hired to run the place. They all wore black t-shirts with the letters TVL printed on the left breast in gold. The girls wore sexy little black shorts or skin- tight leggings. The guys and Kathy wore black slacks. Kathy had a clipboard in one hand. Like the others, she was watching Reese and waiting for him to speak.

As difficult as it was to do, Reese managed to push all the things that were weighting down his conscience to the back of his mind; the baby news, the fact that his uncle Kev was lying in bed at the Villa Taj recovering from being shot four times, the fact that his father had died on the same floor that he was now standing on. He had to keep business first. It's what his father would have done.

He handed the blunt and his cup to Chubb and then swept his eyes around the large square room. There were several hundred circular tables on the highly polished hardwood floor, a black- curtained stage on the east wall where music artists would perform, a mechanical bull-riding machine beneath the DJ booth on the far left of the back wall, and on the opposite side of that wall was a glass-floored VIP section which jutted out over a section of wall that had an artificial backdrop for those who wished to take photographs inside of the club. The door in the middle of the back wall opened to a staircase that led up to the second floor VIP section and a third-floor office, which explained the ten-feet wide tinted window thirty feet above the door. Passed down from father to son, Cup's old office was now Reese's office.

"We got a photographer?" Reese asked.

"Yes, sir, we do have a photographer," Kathy said, turning and pointing at one of the most beautiful dark-skinned girls Reese had ever seen. "Her name's Raven. When I last talked to your assistant I told her I had taken care of that. Raven is also in charge of The Visionary Lounge's social media pages."

"Glad to be a part of the team, sir," Raven chirped.

"Glad to have you," Reese replied with a nod. "In fact, I'm glad to have you all." He moved closer to the two lines of employees, taking in their faces. "I don't have some long, drawn out speech to give, but I assure you that the reopening of this club is very important to me. My fatherloved this club. He loved everything about it. Whenever I needed to talk to him about something,this is where I usually found him."

He began to walk along the lines of employees. "Now, I'm not a strict boss, but Kathy is-- it's why I hired her in the first place. I expect every single one of you to perform your duties professionally and respectfully. Keep the drama at home. This isn't some reality show and I won't tolerate it being treated like one. Respect my father's legacy by respecting each other. Any and all drama queens will be fired immediately. We clear on that?"

A monotonous echo of 'yes sirs' accompanied by forty-nine head nods ensued. Kathy's head was the only one that didn't nod and Reese was okay with that.

He glanced at his watch. "Okay, it's a quarter past noon. Over the next two or three days I'll be meeting with all of you in my office for fifteen minutes each." He paused, thinking. "On second thought, we'll do this two at a time so we can get all the introductions out of the way before the doors open at nine. We'll get started around two o'clock. Kathy, you come up to my office now so we can do some catching up. See you all in a few."

Reese turned and headed toward the back door, pulling out

his iPhone as he went. He was about to send and email to Chance the Rapper to make sure that he was still going to perform his scheduled five-song set tonight, but a text from an unfamiliar number stopped him in his tracks.

Ay, this BK. Gimme a call. I'm in Chiraq for the wknd.

Reese was frowning at the text as they walked into his office. He sat down at his Honduran mahogany wood desk, still frowning, still urging his mind to come up with a person he knew with the initials B.K., a person whose cell phone had a 219 area code.

Kathy cleared her throat. "Reese?"

"My bad," he said, looking up from his phone. "Fill me in. Anything I need to know before we start this party?"

"Yes," Kathy said. "I believe there is. First and foremost, I'd like to thank you for allowing me to do this my way because I wouldn't have it any other way. Secondly, I just got off the line with Chance's people. He'll be in early to go over his routine and so will the others."

The "others" was a long list of Chicago music artists who had all volunteered to come out and support the club's reopening event. Reese had everyone from Twista and the Speedknot Mobstaz to newer artists like Dreezy, Chance the Rapper, and Sicko Mobb scheduled to hit the stage tonight. Tomorrow night he had Lil Durk, Grindo, 2 Chainz and Boosie performing, followed by another night of star-studded performances.

Reese grabbed his Styrofoam from Chubb, leaned back in his chair, and gave his attention toKathy as she ran through a list of wants, needs, gripes, and complaints. To be forty, she wasquite attractive with big, brown eyes, flawless cocoa skin, and a sweet, easy smile. Inside, she was tougher than nails. She was a longtime friend of his mom and before Cup's death she had managed both The Visionary Lounge and Redbone's for an entire year and a half. Then, while getting dressed on morning she had discovered a lump in her breast. When her doctor confirmed it was breast cancer she gave up her jobs to focus on fighting the disease. It had taken a lot of chemo therapy and prescription medications, but she had won the battle. Now, she was cancer- free and back on the job looking even stronger than before. Once had to admire her strength.

It took her more than twenty minutes to finish going over the notes she'd jotted down on herclipboard. She wanted iPads, cosmetics for the girls, an espresso machine and a bigger television in the employee break room, and four company vehicles to pick up and drop off employees who might otherwise have a hard time getting to and from work. It was a reasonable yet ridiculous wish-list that Reese wouldn't think about until Kathy brought it up again at a later date. He thanked her and excused her from his office.

Chubb and Suwu left out behind her, only instead of trailing her back out onto the club floor they turned right at the bottom of the staircase and went out the rear exit into the parking lot; Reese watched them from the camera monitor on his desk. Barely three minutes had passed when a small red BMW Coupe pulled into the parking lot. A woman emerged from the BMW and the two large men escorted her up to the door of Reese's office. They stayed out in the hallway and she came into the office, scantily clad in a skimpy red dress and stiletto heels.

Biting down on the corner of her lower lip, she pushed the door shut with the tip of a forefinger.

Reese stood up, took off his shades, and set them down next to his phone. "So," he said, moving toward her, "I assume I'm the one o'clock dentist's appointment you mentioned to Shawnna."

"Shut up," Myesha said with a laugh as she reached out to

use his tie like a leash, yanking him to her. She kissed him hard on the lips. "How long do we have before I leave?"

He checked his watch. "Til two. That gives us about an hour and ten minutes. Where'd Shawnna go?"

"She went home. Said she's gonna take a nap, think about the baby. I can't believe you actually got her pregnant. Do you have any idea how long her and Dawn have been my best friends? Years, Reese. Since elementary."

Reese put his hands on her soft, round butt and pulled her in tight. "We can make this our last time if you want to. I can't lie, I feel kinda bad about it myself. Especially with her being pregnant."

"No. No, I don't want this to be our last time."

"We can't just keep fucking like this, creeping around and shit. What if she finds out?""She won't find out."

"I don't know." Reese was saying one thing, but his body was betraying him. His hands were stuck to Myesha's butt and his dick was hard. "I don't know what we should do. I know what I wanna do right now, though."

"Really? And what's that?" She was already unzipping his pants."Take care of whatever dental work you need done."

Myesha squatted quickly. She pulled his dick out of the zipper hole in his pants, threw her head back, and extended her tongue. "Ahh. See any cavities?" she joked.

The jokes were over as far as Reese was concerned. He moved forward, held his dick in one hand and guided it right down her throat. Myesha didn't have a gag reflex. It was something Reese had learned during their first sexual encounter at his Burr Ridge mansion shortly after the murder of Lee Wilkins, Jr., when Shawnna had started staying at her father's house. Rubbing on Myesha's ass one night in his recording studio had led to her sucking his dick, initiating a month and a half long affair right under her best friend's nose.

He tried not to think about his pregnant girlfriend and the bond she shared with Myesha. He leaned back on his desk and watched Myesha give him the ultimate porn star treatment, swearingto himself that this was going to be his last time with this beautiful woman and at the same time knowing that it wouldn't be. Myesha was the epitome of a bad bitch. Chubb had once said that Myesha--with her short blonde hair and killer curves--was the "Chicago Amber Rose" and the guys still used the name to describe her when she wasn't around.

In an effort to avoid a premature ejaculation, Reese clamped a hand under Myesha's chinand lifted. She stood up, smiling the most seductive smile she had in her arsenal of smiles, and bent over his desk.

"You got a condom?" Reese asked, unbuckling his belt.

"Oh, now you wanna use protection? After how many times?""One baby is enough for me."

"I'm on the pill anyway. My body is what pays the bills. Nobody wants to see a pregnantstripper."

Reese unbuttoned his pants and gave them and his boxer briefs a push that sent them downto his ankles.

"You should wear suits more often," Myesha said, looking back at him.

"Really? You like it?" He slipped his erection into her and took a couple of seconds to revel in the warmth of her tight pussy before he began fucking her the way he always did--fast and hard.

Myesha said, "Yes," about a hundred times over the next thirty minutes and Reese had no idea if she was answering his question or not, but he assumed that she did indeed like the suit.

Chapter 24

"Luke said hi," Dawn said as she sat down next to Shawnna at their dining room table. She'd bought Italian beef sandwiches and french fries for both of them and was peeling the paper wrapping off of her sandwich before her butt even made contact with her chair. "He's in Houston with Deja and D-Boy on some kind of promo tour. I think it's for the album they're about to release in October. God, I love that couple, you know? They make good music together, they look good together. Luke got us front row tickets to their show at the United Center on the eleventh, if you wanna go. And he said congrats on the baby."

"How does your boyfriend know I'm pregnant?" "Beats me." Dawn cracked a smile.

"Beat you? Is that what you want me to do?"

Dawn shook her head no as she took a huge bite out of her sandwich. She chewed and chewed. Watching her identical twin sister chew up the bite of sandwich, Shawnna shook her head, laughed, and then went back to thumbing through the photo gallery on her iPhone, casting starry-eyed gazes at every photo she'd taken with Reese.

Although she had the mind to knock Dawn upside the head for the old needle-in-the-condom trick, Shawnna was more than happy to have a baby growing in her belly. She had already started on a list of people she would invite to the shower. The first three names on the list were her and Dawn's closest friends: Myesha, Tamera, and Tirzah. The four other names on her list of invitees were girls she'd gone to school with and she knew the list would lengthen in the coming weeks.

A selfie she'd taken of her and Reese sharing a kiss in the backseat of his Phantom caught her eye and brought a smile to her face. Deep down (though she would never admit it to anyone, not even to herself) she was hoping that Reese would propose to her before the baby was born. Ifthere was one thing she did not want to be it was a single mom. But Reese was rich--filthy rich-- and Shawnna was almost certain that he was nowhere near ready to settle down. It's why she'd turned down his request to have her move in with him. In her mind, a ring meant commitment to building a family. Without a ring she felt safer staying in her father's building.

"You need to eat," Dawn said, shoving the plastic bag with the food in it over to Shawnna.

"You're eating for two now."

"Myesha made tacos," Shawnna said.

"Where is she? She was supposed to come and kick it with us at the shop.""She had to go to the dentist."

"Why'd she have to go to the dentist?"

"Fuck if I know," Shawnna replied, putting her phone down. "I told Reese. He said he was happy about it, but he didn't look happy."

"Maybe he was higher than he usually is."

Shawnna chuckled. "That's exactly what he said, too."

"See? High minds think alike." Dawn's eyes were redder than Rudolph's shiny nose. "Wait 'til Mama gets off work. She's gonna go nuts."

"Jesus Christ, Dawn. Don't tell me you told her too." "Okay, I won't tell you."

"Will you ever learn how to keep a secret?"

"Mmm-mmm." Dawn was chewing up another big mouthful of bread and beef, so an 'mmm-mmm' was all she could manage.

Outside of the dining room windows a flash of lightening illuminated the sky. Thunder then crackled. Shawnna jumped, but Dawn didn't glance up at the sound. It was as though she hadn't heard. Shawnna didn't need to look out of a window to know it had started raining; she could hear it and smell it in the air.

"You've got two heads waiting on you at the shop," Dawn said. "Want me to tell them you're not coming back in today or what?"

"No, I'm going back in with you. It's a busy day and these are the days we need to be working the hardest. We're a new shop. Gotta build up our clientele so we won't need Daddy's money."

"The only reason we got so much business this weekend is because The Visionary Lounge is about to be crackin' all weekend long. That and the Deja and D-Boy concert Sunday night."

"Then we need to be in the shop all fucking weekend with our hair stylists getting to the money. Every dollar counts."

"For real," Dawn said, stuffing ten fries into her greedy mouth.

Just then, someone began ringing their doorbell again and again like some kind of lunatic. Dawn and Shawnna looked at each other.

"Who the fuck is that?" Shawnna asked, standing up and reaching to the middle of the table where she'd left her black Gucci purse. She had a fully loaded .44 Bulldog revolver inside of the purse. She went to the living room, holding her purse by its straps, and stopped at the window that overlooked the front porch. Dawn as at her side a second later, washing down the fries with an orange-flavored Crush soda. The blinds were shut.

The doorbell kept ringing and over the drizzling sound of rain they heard voices--female voices. There were at least four or five of them.

"Dawn! Bitch, whoever you are, you need to come on out here and take what's coming to you 'cause I ain't leaving until you do."

The twins looked at each other again, their heads cocked to the side and brows knitted. "Somebody got me fucked up," Dawn said.

"No," Shawnna replied, "somebody got *us* fucked up.""It's been a while since we last whooped a bitch." "Yep. Shaila was the last one."

"No, it was Chandra, at the strip club, remember?"

Shawnna snapped her thumb and middle finger together and nodded her head as they walked to the door. "Damn. You're right. How could I forget that beat-down we gave Chandra?"

They stopped at the closet beside the front door and Shawnna exchanged her Louis Vuittonheels for a pair of Nike running shoes.

The doorbell was still ringing.

"Don't jump in," Dawn said. "Not unless they try to jump me.""Yeah. Sure. Whatever you say, Sis."

Shawnna turned the doorknob. Dawn went out first. Their apartment was on the secondfloor, so Dawn had time to remove her earrings and hand them to Shawnna before they reached the square-tiled vestibule. Dawn didn't hesitate to snatch open the porch door and confront her opponent.

The girl at the forefront of the five-girl crew was large and obviously in charge. She was tall and fat with a charcoal complexion and a tight little ponytail sticking out from the left side of herhead. Her sky blue Nike shirt looked old; the white Nike swoosh across the chest was peeling in some places. Her shoulders were damp from the rain. She seemed poor, but her appearance was much more cleaned up than that of her four disciples.

"Which one of you hoes is Dawn?" the big girl asked."Who wanna know?" Dawn retorted.

"Big Wanda wanna know," said the big girl who looked like someone who might be named Big Wanda.

"Well, I'm Dawn and I have never heard of a bitch named Big Wanda.""Yeah, but I bet you heard of my baby daddy."

"And who exactly is he?"

"The nigga you've been riding around with. Luther. Luke." Big Wanda produced a smartphone and showed Dawn a photo.

Sure enough, it was Luke, all hugged up with Big Wanda in somebody's backyard withthree little boys smiling up at them.

Neither of the Wilkins twins were surprised to see the three children; Luke was a proud father, always showing off photos of his sons. But he'd told them that the mother of his children was in prison for stabbing some girl at a party two years ago, a girl she'd suspected he was fucking when she wasn't around.

"Okay," Shawnna said from behind Dawn, "why in the fuck are you over here ringing our doorbell? My sister ain't got shit to do with you and your baby-daddy issues. Take that up with him."

"For real though," Dawn added, stepping back to shut the door.

Big Wanda lunged at Dawn, closing the fat fingers of her left hand in Dawn's blond-dyed hair and cocking back with the other hand. At the same time, the other four girls rushed in tohelp their bear-sized leader.

"You big bitch," Shawnna muttered as she hastily drew the revolver from her purse, pointed it at Big Wanda, and blasted a hole in the big girl's right shoulder.

Blood sprayed from Big Wanda's back and mixed in with the rainfall behind her. The four friends scrambled backward and leaped from the porch so quickly that Shawnna had no chance to take aim at them. Big Wanda stumbled sideways down the porch's concrete steps. The fat fingers she'd balled into Dawn's hair were now pressed flat over the eye-sized hole in the right shoulder of her ancient sky blue Nike shirt.

"I tried to warn you, fat girl," Shawnna said. "Better take that big bad bully shit to another set of twins 'cause these two bitches ain't goin' for it. And that's on my dead brother."

An old Buick Park Avenue had been left running in the middle of the street, its driver's door left hanging open, no doubt by the overweight mother who was no hurrying towards it with a gaping hole in her shoulder.

"My fucking ear is ringing," Dawn said, rubbing her left ear as they watched Big Wanda drive herself away in the Buick.

"The only thing that needs to be ringing right now is Luke's phone," Shawnna said. "He needs to be explaining to me why I just had to shoot a bitch!"

Chapter 25

The sex that had begun on Lakita "Bubbles" Thomas's living room sofa had led to the floor in front of the sofa, to the hallway (with her bent at the waist with her hands on the wall like some suspected armed robber being patted down by police and Juice behind her pounding his foot-long pole in and out of her as though he intended to split her in two), and finally to her king bed where it ended doggy-style with his cum sliding down into the crack of her jiggling butt cheeks.

A much needed nap followed the hour-long sexathon. Bubbles fell asleep with her jaw on his chest, which is how she awoke at a little after 3:00. After shaking him awake, she went to the bathroom and freshened up. When she came out he went in. By 4:00 they were back in the Jaguar SUV on their way back to the mean inner-city streets of Chicago.

Juice's iPhone had died. He plugged it up to the charger and started texting on his flip- phone. Bubbles kept glancing over at him as she drove. She felt like she'd won the lotto with Lee Wilkins Sr. at her side. She hadn't been back to work at the strip club in weeks, ever since the day she'd gone to his house with Myesha and ended up shooting a masked teenager with a shotgun. Having a handsome black man of her own to love and cater to, to depend on and argue with, and ultimately submit her mind and body to every waking moment of the day was all she'd ever hoped and prayed for and Juice was the answer to those prayers. Her only real fear regarding their relationship was that he might one day grow tired of her and move on to another woman. What if this thing they had was, in his mind, nothing more than a fling, something he was using to get over his recent divorce?

"What do I mean to you?" she asked, hoping she wouldn't sound too desperate for his love. He looked at her. "What do you think you mean to me?"

"I'm not sure. That's why I asked."

Juice hesitated. "Look," he said finally, "I ain't into that Romeo and Juliet type of poetic love shit, aight? But, I'll tell you this much: I think, at first you was just a stripper with a big booty that I wanted to fuck, but now it's different. Now it's a lot different."

"Different how?"

"You're more than just a bad bitch with a sexy body. You're a good woman who's raising a beautiful little girl, and you're a good mother to her. You carry yourself the way I believe all black women should--with morals, values, you know? Head held high. And best of all, you're independent. Got that big ass house, a Mercedes. I know that's just material wealth, but it's your and it's all in your name. That's a huge accomplishment. Most females I grew up with ain't even got a car."

"I know you just got divorced and all," Bubbles said as she drove down a winding, tree- lined road, "but could you ever see yourself getting married again…if you found the right woman?"

"Of course I can."

It occurred to Bubbles that Juice hadn't been faithful to his ex-wife. She knew of at least two women he'd cheated with, one of whom was Candy, one of the dancers Bubbles worked with at Redbone's.

"What about being faithful?" Bubbles asked. "Not trying to dig up dirt from your past, but I know like everybody else knows that you had some bitches on the side. I guess my question is, and let me stop beating around the bush, would you ever cheat on me? I mean, if we were to get married. I just wanna know."

"No," he said, shaking his head. "I only cheated a handful

of times with Chandra and once with Chandra and Candy. I regret it, but knowing now that Chandra's mom and my ex-wife were already on some down-low lesbian shit before I ever even thought about fucking Chandra, I don't feel like I was wrong. I wouldn't do it again, though."

"I sure in the hell hope not."

"We need to stop at a liquor store once we make it back into the city.""What liquor store? Any liquor store?"

"Nuh-uh." Juice opened the flip-phone and pressed a few buttons. "Cardinal Wine and Spirits, the one on Central Avenue."

"And what exactly will we be doing there?"

"Just picking up some boxes for Reese. You know The Visionary Lounge reopens tonight. He wants everything to be perfect. Pulling out all the stops, I guess." He shrugged.d "I'm just helping."

"Forgive me for not believing you," Bubbles said, flicking another glance at him. She'd been around him long enough to know that he was more secretive than an American spy in North Korea when it came down to his drug deals. The one thing that always gave him away was the use of the prepaid flip-phone; he had bought four of them in the short time since they'd began dating and each time he got a new one he broke the old one.

"You wanna stop by The Visionary Lounge?" Juice asked. "It opens at nine but we can get in early and meet Chance the Rapper if you want to."

"I like him," Bubbles said. "He puts a positive spin on things. Our kids need that kind of hope."

"Yeah, I like his music too. That's why I asked if you wanted to stop by there…before we catch that flight."

Bubbles gasped and smiled. "A flight?"

"Don't act all surprised. You threatened me to book that

damn trip, so that's what I'm aboutto do."

"Oh please. Nobody threatened you. It was a simple request."

"Do I need to start recording our conversations?" he asked. "Because it's quite obvious thatsomething is going wrong with your memory."

With a growing smile, Bubbles grasped his left hand and brought it up to her lips. She kissedthe hand twice; he snatched it back before she could land a third smooch.

"Keep your sneaky lips off me," Juice said with a chuckle.

"While you're talking about my memory," Bubbles said, chuckling with him and ignoring her iPhone as it buzzed with a call from Myesha, "let's not forget who's about to be a grandparent. Grandpa Juice."

"If Reese wasn't Cup's son and my nephew's nephew I would've shot him the first time I caught him fucking my daughter."

"You actually *saw* them doing it?""Long story."

Bubbles laughed. "Why didn't you shoot Kobe? I mean, he was with her for half of thisyear. And if I'm not mistak--" Cut off by the incessant buzzing of her iPhone as it began ringing again, she made a growling noise in her throat. "Hold one second so I can answer this because she'll just keep calling if I don't." She answered it on speakerphone. "What's up?"

"Who you with? Juice?" Myesha asked.

"Yes, I am with my man." Bubbles smiled at him, proud to have a boss like Juice all to herself.

"Tell him he needs to turn on his phone ASAP because shit is going down. The police just found a dead body in the trunk of Kobe's car and they think it's him. Girl, you know it's about tobe some more shit with the Breeds about that. But bitch, the real story is--wait, put me onspeaker so Juice can hear this."

"You're on speaker," Bubbles told her. "I hear you," Juice said.

"Y'all remember Big Wanda? Ol' girl Luke got the kids by?" Myesha asked.

"Of course." Juice nodded, slipping the flip-phone back into his pocket. "I know her. She stabbed Brianna in the chest over Luke, damn near killed that girl."

"Well," Myesha said, dragging out the word. "Big Wanda got out of jail the day before yesterday and I guess she's still caught up on Luke or whatever. She showed up at the twins' front door, ringing the bell like crazy and shouting for Dawn to come outside and fight."

Juice sat up straight in his seat. His eyelids, which had been at half-mast, flew up like window shades. He listened intently while turning on is iPhone.

"Big Wanda grabbed Dawn by the hair," Myesha continued, "and the raggedy hoes she had with her tried to jump in, but Shawnna put a stop to the fight before it went anywhere. She shot Big Wanda in the shoulder. The other bitches took off running and Big Wanda drove herself to the hospital. They say she's in critical condition. I just hung up from talking to Shawnna. Her crazy ass is right back in the salon with Dawn like she didn't just shoot a bitch. Not to mention the fact that she's God knows how many weeks pregnant. I can only imagine how the rest of this weekend is gonna turn out."

"However it turns out," Bubbles said, "I better not be here to see it." She looked at Juice as he dialed Shawnna's number and hoped that the Big Wanda incident wouldn't spoil their plans.

Chapter 26

The weekend getaway plan was history as far as Juice was concerned. His daughters took precedence over his relationship with Bubbles. There were no two people in the world that he loved more than Dawn and Shawnna Wilkins. The loss of his son had only served to deepen his undying love for the twins.

He FaceTimed Shawnna and got Dawn instead.

"You should really start keeping your phone on at all times," Dawn said with a thumbnail between her teeth and her eyes not looking at Juice but at something in front of her. "I must havecalled you ten times."

"Battery was dead," Juice explained. "Where's your sister?"

"In the bathroom. She got sick again. That baby's already kicking her butt. I'm standing at the window in the shop."

"Get away from the window."

"Shawnna wants me to watch out for her, in case the cops come."

"Get away from the window," Juice repeated in a firmer tone. "I know this may come as abit of a surprise to you, but you and Shawnna look a lot alike."

Stone-faced, Dawn looked at the phone--at Juice--and moved away from the window."Don't do me," she said.

"What makes you think Wanda's people won't come through there with guns spraying? Come on, Dawn. I know you got better sense than that." He pulled out the flip-phone. "I want you and Shawnna to sit in that office we talked in earlier until I get there. I gotta make a quick pitstop, but I'll be there in the next thirty minutes or so. I'm about to send some security over there now, so y'all should be good." He was texting Wayno.

"Let me call you back," Dawn said. "Luke's on the other line.""Tell him to call me as soon as you finish talking to him."

"Okay. I'll call you back from my phone," Dawn said and hung up.

Juice took a moment to breathe. They were in the city and Bubbles was trying to see if she had what it took to become the first black female NASCAR driver. When she turned ontoCentral Avenue she almost hit a van.

"Slow the fuck down!" Juice snapped, holding the dashboard with both hands."Oh." Bubbles chuckled one. "My bad. Thought you were in a hurry."

"Not to go to my goddamn grave."

"I like this truck so much. I didn't even know Jaguar made SUVs. This motherfucker isdope. It's so fast. I love it."

Juice shook his head. He got a reply on the flip-phone. The gang was getting ready to strap up and head over to the hair salon. He thanked Wayno and told him that he'd be there shortly.

"So, where are you taking me?" Bubbles asked. "Or is it a surprise?""Driver's Ed," Juice said.

"Very funny."

"A vacation is the last thing on my mind right now. My daughter just shot somebody. She's my top priority."

Bubbles sucked her teeth and gave him a look, but she didn't say anything. A minute later she steered the sporty silver SUV on big chrome rims into the parking lot in front of Cardinal Wine and Spirits. Juice pointed at a black Mercedes G-Wagon and told her to park next to it. Shedid it without a fuss or a tight-eyed look. He reached around to the floor behind his seat, hooked his fingers under the straps of a cheap, black duffle bag, and pulled it onto his lap.

"I'll be right back," he said to Bubbles, who was texting someone on her phone.

Bubbles didn't look up or say anything so he just shoved open his door and got out. Walking around the front of his

SUV, he gave the hood a playful slap, but there was still no reaction from Bubbles. He shook his head and turned his eyes to the grinning Mexican man behind the wheel of the G-Wagon. Hector Ortega's orange button-up shirt was covered with palm trees and it wasn't buttoned; his hairy chest was exposed as well as his thin gold necklace and thick gold cross pendant. He reached across the passenger's seat and threw open the door for Juice.

"What it look like, old man?" Juice asked as he got in and swung the door shut.

Hector leaned forward over the steering wheel, peering at the sky which had grown darkwith storm clouds. "Looks like a storm's coming, is what it looks like." He turned back to Juice and they shook hands. "Look at you, Juice. You're gaining back the gut you got rid of in the joint. Old lady must be feeding you good, eh?"

"I got divorced last month," Juice said."You shitting me?"

"Swear to god." Juice held up his right hand, palm out, and then slapped the palm on the top of the duffle before unzipping it to reveal the rubber-banded stacks of cash that were stuffed inside of it. "This is all of it. Gave you damn near all the big bills this time, too. Mostly just hundreds and fifties."

"You know, Juice, I gotta hand it to you. You're the best hustler I've ever met. The other guys I deal with don't have a clue how truly fucking blessed they are to even know some-body like me. Gracie--he's another guy we did time with in Stateville, one of the Black P-Stones, not sure if you ever got to meet him--that dumb fuck caught a DUI out in Crystal Lake when he was leaving some chick's house. Cops arrested him, towed his car, and found four kilos in the trunk. Can you believe that *dumb fuck* actually had his mom call me asking to borrow money for a lawyer? I broke that phone so fast. Didn't even bother hanging up, just broke it while she was still talking, then walked out to my shed and took a hammer to it."

"They won't be getting you, huh?" Juice laughed. Part of him wanted to sit there and listen to the old guy, but the other part knew that getting to the hair salon with his daughters was imperative.

"Guys like Gracie, my niece's boyfriend Loco, a guy I met through Gracie who goes by the name of Rocky--none of them will ever get more than five bricks at a time from me. And I do mean ever. Lazy fucks couldn't sell a cat to an old lady. You, on the other hand…you're fucking special. You're a whole 'nother fucking genre. Hell, ten bricks won't last you a day. Forty'll be gone in a week."

Hector's math was off by about a week in the latter calculation. It had actually taken Juice two weeks to sell the forty kilos he'd gotten from Hector the evening before Kev was shot. He'd paid $380,000.00 for the first twenty and Hector had fronted him the other twenty kilos, which was why he was sitting there with another $380,000.00 on his lap.

"Yeah, I had to go hard this time," Juice said. "I got robbed a few weeks ago. Had to make up for the loss. But, I'm done for a while now. Figure I might as well back out before I get caught up in some kinda bust. Getting too old to be doing bids. I'm about to be a granddaddy soon."

"Grandkids are a good thing. Love mine to death."

"I can't wait." Juice made a show of checking his watch. "I got somewhere to be in a few minutes, so I guess I'll see you later." He hoisted the duffle over his seat, intending to set it down on the back seat, but there were already two extra large black duffle bags stacked one on top of the other resting on the seat. He changed courses and lowered his duffle bag to the floor instead.

"Wait," Hector said.

"Wait?" Juice repeated. "Wait for what?"

"I got a deal for you. A deal so sweet you could drop it in a trick-or-treater's pumpkin bucket."

"Nah, I'm good. Shits too hot in my neighborhood. Police everywhere you turn. I can't risk going back to the joint, not when I got a pregnant daughter--" Juice cast another glance at his watch-- "who I need to be getting to right now."

"Just hear me out, Juice. Just hear me out. Okay?" Juice nodded impatiently.

"My niece's boyfriend…Loco…I want that motherfucker dead. He stole twelve kilos from me a few days ago. I even have the dumb fuck on video doing it."

"So? Have one of your guys do it."

"That's the thing, my friend. That's the thing right there. You see, Loco's a Latin King. His guys are my guys. You see the guys in that gray Riviera parked by the entrance? And the guys inthe old Caddy two spaces away from the Riviera?"

The parking lot's entrance was on Hector's side of the G-Wagon. All Juice had to do was move his eyes an inch to the right of Hector's wrinkled forehead to see the Hispanics in the Riviera. Another inch and he was looking at a Sedan DeVille full of Mexicans. He inched his eyes back over to Hector's. "I see 'em. What's that, your security?"

"They're my security and also Loco's security. He's one of their top guys so getting one of them to take him out would be suicide on my part. See what I'm saying? Even asking, youknow? That's why I need you to get it done for me. Those two duffles back there." Hector arced a thumb towards the backseat. "You got thirty bricks in there, fifteen in each bag. They're all yours if you get that dumb fuck Loco whacked. I'll give you his address, his mother's address-- anything you need."

Juice was tempted to take the offer. He knew a hundred young niggas who would get the job done for a quarter of a kilo. The rest he could hold on to until the streets were begging for good coke. Then, he could sell the kilos for $34,000.00 apiece, maybe even more. He could easily add a million dollars to his fortune. Easily.

"I'll think it over," Juice said, opening his door.

"Take the duffles," Hector urged ."If you don't they'll know I'm up to something. Hit me later on the burner phone. I'll come and get them back from you if you don't wanna take the deal."

Juice took the two duffle bags.

Chapter 27

The turn up was real inside of Shawnna's office at Supreme Hair. Myesha had arrived with party supplies: two big bottles of Hennessy and an aluminum foil-covered bowl of weed brownies. During the last bite of her second brownie, Dawn decided that there wouldn't be a third. Not for her at least. She could deal with the cognac, but not the brownies.

A Bulletface song featuring Gucci Mane was playing. Shawnna, who was sober but equally turnt, was twerking with Tamera and Tirzah whom Dawn had called in as backups in case Wanda's crew returned for a fight. Myesha was refilling cups and recording video footage of the turn up for Snapchat and Instagram. It was a good thing that there were six other stylists workingat Supreme Hair on this busy Friday afternoon. If not for them, business would have been at a stand still.

A knock at the door settled them down. Shawnna put a forefinger to her lips to shush the intoxicated bunch as she opened the door and let in the one guy that every girl in NorthLawndale had a crush on: Wayno.

He was clad in all white -- True Religion T-shirt and jeans, Louis Vuitton belt, and AirForce One sneakers. Behind the dreadlocks was a ridiculously handsome face. He had a brown paper grocery bag in one hand, folded down at the top so you couldn't see what was in it. But Dawn knew what was in it. Cash. Her father's cash; today's take from the drugs sold in that particular neighborhood. A diamond-encrusted watch was wrapped tightly around Wayno's left wrist. For a moment Dawn stood still, training her gaze on Wayno. She waited for him to lookher way. He did. He looked at her and a little smile began to play around the corners of his mouth.

"Boy, if I wasn't married," Tirzah said, eyeing him over her cup. "I'm not married," Myesha said, raising her hand as if volunteering.

He chuckled, stepping in and closing the door. To Shawnna he said, “I got the gang outfront. Your pops told us to come and kick it here. Said he’ll be here in a few.” He walked around to the swivel chair behind Shawnna’s desk and sat down. The brown paper bag went under the desk.

“I think Dawn wants to fuck you,” Shawnna said.

“No I don’t!” Dawn lied.

“We all wanna fuck you,” Myesha said and offered him a cup of iced cognac.

“I’m cool,” Wayno said with a sexy grin. “Y’all crazy. Dawnna and Shawn, can I talk to y’all in private?”

Dawn squinted. “It’s Shawnna and Dawn, not Dawnna and Shawn.”“He said that bullshit on purpose,” Shawnna accused.

Wayno said nothing. He smiled neutrally, rocking back and forth to the music. Myesha filed out of the room ahead of Tamera and Tirzah. Out of the corner of his eye he watched the three ofthem leave. Dawn didn’t care. She couldn’t blame him for looking. It was to be expected. They were bad bitches with fat asses just like her and Shawnna. Any man would have looked.

“Take that stupid smile off your face,” Shawnna said, folding her arms over her breasts and leaning a hip against the side of her desk. “What the hell do you want?”

Instead of leaving his face, Wayno’s smile grew wider--wide enough to show his teeth. “I always heard pregnancy made women evil. Didn’t know it started so soon, though.” He leaned his head back and shut his eyes.

Now every face in the office wore a smile.

“I done already shot one bitch today,” Shawnna said. “What’s that supposed to mean?” Wayno asked. “You know what it means.”

“Why did you shoot that girl anyway?”

"Because her and the dirty little bitches she brought with her tried to jump my sister right in front of me. Because the bitch was so big I thought she was Tyler Perry in a new costume--Dirty Madea or some shit. Because I just lost my brother two months ago and I'm not about to lose the only sibling I have left. Shall I go on?"

"Preach, sister," Dawn chimed in. She was in front of the desk, her thighs pressed against it as she leaned forward, nostrils sucking in the smell of Wayno's cologne. She realize that she was halfway drunk and pissed at Luke for the Big Wanda debacle and she wondered which one of those circumstances was responsible for her wanting to ride Wayno's dick right there in the chairhe was sitting in.

He opened his eyes and looked from Dawn to Shawnna then from Shawnna to Dawn.

Dawn took a step back, not wanting to appear as sexually hungry as she felt on the inside.

"I wasn't siding with Wanda," he said, turning a full circle in the swivel. "Damn. Don't attack me. Y'all going to The Visionary Lounge tonight?"

"I'm going," Shawnna said.

"I haven't decided yet," Dawn answered, "but I'll probably go if she goes."

"What ever y'all do, don't go to Club Stadium," Wayno said, just as the door opened and Juice came walking in. He picked up the paper bag and gave it to Juice. "You walked in right when I was telling them. Make sure you don't go to Club Stadium out in Markham tonight. I talked to Kaira, the chick who asked about the money on Darren's head. She said he'll be at Stadium tonight, him and some of his guys. We'll already be there when he pulls up. He ain't gon' make it out of his car."

Juice threw his right arm around Dawn's lower back and pulled her in close to his side. His other arm did the same thing to Shawnna. Dawn had the distinct feeling that he was making a nonverbal statement to Wayno: *These two are off limits*, his eyes seemed to say. He turned to Shawnna and gave her a stern look.

"I know, Daddy. I know," Shawnna said.

"You and your sister…" He didn't finish. He didn't need to.

Chapter 28

Darren and Kaira stood on the balcony of his hotel room at The Wit looking out over downtown Chicago. The smoke from his blunt drifted, mellowing in the air, keeping the mosquitoes at a safe distance. His Robin's jeans and shirt were a cool aqua and the sky was a deeper, truer blue. It was a pleasant combination.

"I don't know about you," Kaira said, watching him closely, arms folded across her chest. "My girl Shaila told me a lot about you before she got killed."

"Shaila was good people. We fucked around at one point. She lived downstairs from where Iused to live."

Kaira sighed. "How'd she die?" "She got shot by somebody." "And you don't know who did it?"

"What the fuck I look like, a detective? How am I supposed to know who killed her? Probably the same individuals who killed my nigga Big Jay's sister, my nigga Cash Boy, my nigga RoRo-G, and a bunch of other niggas from my block. This is Chicago. Niggas get killed every day."

Kaira shook her head and strode back into the room. Her body was the reason she was so popular on Instagram. She wore a white T-shirt that stopped two inches above her pierced navel, white capri leggings, and white six-inch pumps. Darren suspected her butt was fake. Maybe the titties were too. She had lush eyebrows and a cute brown face with hair as long and straight as a horse's tail.

They had company. Darren had picked up Markus and Darius, two of his older cousins, before going to meet up with Kaira. The two were brothers, Gangster Disciples from the farsouth side, who'd recently moved to the west side with their mother after their south side home was burned down in an overnight fire. They were rolling blunts at the table between the two queen beds, drinking straight from a bottle of Patron, and watching a movie on the wall-mountedtelevision.

Kaira had her own bottle of Patron and after grabbing it and disconnecting her smartphone from her charger, she returned to Darren's side on the balcony. "Want a sip?" she asked, holdingout the bottle to him.

He puffed his blunt and looked at the Chicago skyline. "Nah, you go ahead. I gotta drive tothe club and back. Plus, I got a lot of enemies. Ain't no telling who gon' be there."

"Just do me a favor and don't start shooting at nobody before we get there. Let me out thecar first."

"You said Shaila told you a lot about me?"

"Not a whole lot. Just that you robbed a lot of people, shot some people. That you and your boys were real--you know--gangbangers. That y'all don't play around when it comes to thatstreet shit. It's crazy because she ended up getting killed a few days after that phone call. I never talked to her again." Kaira laughed a nervous laugh. "That's why I said I don't know about you. Niggas like you scare me."

"Ain't no need to be scared of me." Darren turned his head to look at her, exhaling twin streams of smoke from his nostrils. "Shaila was my bitch. I wish I could tell you what happened to her, but we really don't know. If I knew who killed her that nigga would've been dead."

In truth, Darren had murdered Shaila to avoid splitting over fifty thousand dollars with her from a robbery they'd done together. He had walked into her bathroom when she was showering and sprayed her with an AK-47.

He leaned toward Kaira, pressed his lips against her cheek, and put his hand on her ass. "All you gotta worry about is this big boy I got for you."

"Is that so?" She was looking at her phone with the Patron bottle clutched to her chest. "Yeah. What, you don't believe me?"

"You do know I'm in college, right? A bitch got book fees, tuition, rent, and utilities… grocery bills. This high-ass cell phone bill."

"I get it, I get it. How much?" He could see the greed in her eyes and in her smile as she raised the short see-through bottle to her mouth and poured in a shot. The look made him regret posting the photo of his cash to Instagram. Kaira would be there at the nice four-star hotel with him if not for that photo. She was there for the money, not him.

"Five hundred if you want me to stay all night," she said. "Three if we're just fucking for an hour or so."

"Damn, you a prostitute?"

"Boy, don't try me. I have never prostituted a day in my life. It's just that I'm struggling right now and I need a little extra help to pay the bills. I'm not charging you for my pussy. I'm charging you for my presence."

Darren resisted the overwhelming urge to shove Kaira over the balcony. Who did this bitch think she was? Rihanna or somebody? Did she think her pussy was magical? She obviously felt like she was better than him. But that was okay. She would learn. She would learn like Tamiahad learned. Nobody played Darren like a lame and got away with it. Nobody.

He nodded and then glanced meaningfully at his watch. It was a quarter past seven and the sun was waving goodbye. Darren was also waving and pointing at Kaira. "What about cuz and 'em?" Darren asked, squeezing Kaira's soft, perfectly round ass. "Can't leave them out. And don't say no fifteen hundred either."

"That's what it'll be if it's all night. This pussy ain't cheap.""What about from now until we leave out for the club?"

"Nine hundred," Kaira said. "If y'all don't have condoms I brought some. And I don't play the ass games. I'm not licking nobody's asshole and ain't nobody fucking me in mine. As long aswe got that understood we're good to go."

Darren had a thick stack of hundreds in his pocket. He took it out reluctantly and peeled off nine of them. "I'm going first," he said and handed her the bills.

"Fine with me. Oh and I don't do the train thing. One at a time. Only way I'd have a threesome is if it was with two girls and a guy."

Kaira pushed the money down into the Fendi bag under her right arm and got right to it, undoing Darren's Gucci belt buckle. He helped her out by taking the Patron bottle and seconds later she was squatting in front of him, stroking his length in both hands.

"You weren't lying I see," she said and kissed the head of his dick. "It really is a big boy."

If t here was any doubt in Darren's mind that Kaira didn't do this for a living it left the moment she took him into her mouth. It was clear from the start that she knew her way around a dick. She cupped his balls in one hand and jerked his dick with the other while sucking it in and out of her mouth. She looked up at him, smiling around his erection. Saliva gleamed on his length and dripped from her chin. He put his hand on her head and hammered the back of her throat. Her eyes watered, but she didn't stop him. Not even when he went deep and held it there.

They moved into the room and she took off all of her clothes while Darren put on a condom and told his cousins that they could go after him. He made Kaira get on the bed with her face down on a pillow and her ass up in the air. He fucked her that way for a little over twenty minutes and then climbed off the bed and went into the bathroom where he flushed the used condom and lit a Newport before heading back out into the room.

Kaira must have forgotten one of her own rules because she

was doing the train thing. Puffing on his cigarette, Darren sat on the other bed and watched the threesome for a couple of minutes. He might have kept watching if his phone hadn't rang, sending him rushing back out to the balcony to answer the call without the distinct sound of sex in the background.

The caller was Rhonda, Markus and Darius's sister. "Hey cousin," she said, her voice full ofcheer. "Are my brothers with you? Mama said they left with you."

"Yeah. They're busy right now."

"Figured that. I just called their phones. Just tell them I said to call me back before they headto the club. I got a better idea."

"What better idea?" Darren asked.

"Y'all shouldn't go to Club Stadium. Not tonight," Rhonda said."Why not?"

"Because The Visionary Lounge is reopening tonight. That's where everybody's gonna be.

We're getting ready to go now."

"Okay," Darren said, nodding his head. "The Visionary Lounge it is then. We'll be there."

Chapter 29

$1,144,700.00 and thirty kilos of cocaine. Thirty-four kilos if he included the dope he had in the stash-house on Trumbull. That meant he had exceeded his cash goal by almost a hundred and fifty grand. Juice wasn't worried ab out another robbery. The basement windows and first-floor windows had wrought-iron bars over them. The front and back doors wee solid steel. It would take an explosive to get in the first two levels of the building.

Not like a robber would find much cash anyway. Most of it was in the steel safe at his mom's house. He had only $75,000.00 in the building stuffed in a backpack in his bedroom closet. Oh, and there was the $61,580.00 that Wayno had handed him in Shawnna's office which meant he actually had a little over $1.2 million. More than enough to take Bubbles on a nice weekend getaway. Well, Bubbles and the twins. There was no way he was going to leave Shawnna and Dawn in Chicago while the guy who'd murdered his son was still on the loose.

He was thinking about all of this while he stood hunched over the long maple wood table in his dining room, counting the money Wayno had given him for the second time. Wayno stood next to him smoking a cigarette. At the other end of the table Bubbles was FaceTime chatting with her daughter. She still hadn't said a word to Juice since he'd crushed her dreams of a weekend getaway. The twins and their friends were upstairs, presumably getting ready for the club.

"The dumb ass nigga posted where he was going on Instagram," Wayno was saying. "He must think we ain't got no pull in these streets. Kaira sent me the screenshot of his post."

"Just make sure that nigga gets dealt with tonight," Juice said.

"We got him, Big Homie. On God. I'm waiting on Kaira to

text me again. She's with him right now. And she said he picked her up in the same kind of Camaro that pulled up on Kev that night."

"That's what's up. I got another play for you or one of the lil' homies after that. Two whole slabs for one body."

"Two bricks?"

Juice nodded. "My guy wants one of the Latin Kings whacked. Got two keys for the hit. He sent me two addresses and three pictures of the dude. I think it'll be easy money."

"Man, forward that info to me. For two bricks I'll do that shit myself. I don't know a niggain the hood who wouldn't."

"I got you." Juice pulled out the flip-phone and forwarded the messages he'd received from Hector to Wayno's prepaid phone. "Hit my line as soon as it gets handled. I'll get that work rightto you."

After that it got quiet in Juice's apartment. He finished counting the money without interruption, then put it all back in the bag while Wayno took a bathroom break. The relaxing silence was short-lived.

A moment after Wayno had entered the bathroom, the twins came in followed by their three drunken girlfriends. They all seemed to be competing to find out who could laugh the loudest. Dawn was winning. Myesha was in second place.

"Daddy, you are so mean," Dawn said. She walked up behind him and hopped onto hisback. She and Shawnna were going casual tonight in crop-tops, blue jeans, and Louboutin ankle boots.

"How am I mean?" Juice asked, regarding the others suspiciously as they gathered around Bubbles' chair.

"You know how," Shawnna said as she hugged Bubbles with both arms. "What kind of man gets a woman's hopes up for a weekend trip together and then cancels it?"

"A man like your father," Bubbles muttered. She was

off of the phone but she wasn't looking at him. "A selfish, inconsiderate man like Lee over there."

"Okay, first of all," Juice said defensively, "I didn't get nobody's hopes up. I"m not the bad guy."

"We're grown, Daddy," Shawnna said. "You don't need to stay here to watch over us. We are more than capable of fending for ourselves for two or three days. You act like we're stilleight or nine years old."

"Seriously," said the *grown* woman who was perched on her daddy's back like an eight- year-old. "Let us live for once."

"Getcha grown ass off my back," Juice said, rekindling the raucous laughter competition. Then, Wayno returned from the bathroom and all of a sudden the roaring laughter turned into giggles that then became nothing more than batting eyes and lusty gazes. Dawn slippeddown from Juice's back like a kid who'd been caught climbing a forbidden tree. She stalked pastWayno, offering him a busy-fingered wave as she went, as if she was playing an imaginarypiano.

Wayno chuckled coolly. "Y'all don't even need to go to the club. You're already drunk."

"Stop playing," Myesha said, "like you only go to the club to get drunk. Let's be real here.

We all go to the club for the same thing."

"Okay," Juice said, "let's go." He didn't care about Myesha flirting with Wayno. It was the way the twins were looking at Wayno that had him ready to leave.

They all trooped outside and into their vehicles. Tamera and Tirzah had come in a white Mercedes that looked a lot like the one Bubbles owned, only theirs was an E-class. With Shawnna as their designated driver, the five girls piled into the Benz and disappeared down Drake Avenue before Bubbles could even start the F-Pace's engine.

Wayno walked up to Juice's window. "I got the lil' homies

on the way out to Stadium now, but I'm on my way too. You goo? Want me to follow you to The Visionary Lounge first?"

"Nah, you go and get that business handled. That nigga killed my baby boy. He gotta pay forthat."

"Say no more."

Wayno jogged to the waiting Suburban, got in, and sped off just as quickly as Shawnna had. Placing the paper grocery bag full of cash on the floor in front of his seat, Juice turned to

Bubbles. She didn't look at him. She dropped the transmission into drive and pulled off."Baby?" he spoke the her.

No response. "Baby," he repeated.

"I'll go by myself," she said. "I really will. You might be used to dealing with basic bitches who can't afford their own plane tickets, but I'm not anywhere near that category. Hmmm. Believe that. I am a frequent flyer."

"I was just trying to tell you we can go right after the club. Damn.""That's what you better be telling me."

"What?"

"Negro, you heard me. And next time don't take so long to say the shit. Make me a priority--a *top* priority. I changed my whole damn lifestyle to fuck with you. Don't take that shit for granted."

"Baby, calm down." Juice shook his head and, remembering that his son had been gunned down on that very street (they were on 16th Street passing the blinking red lights of Redbone's Gentleman's Club), he drew his .45 Glock and held it on his lap. "We can get right on a plane

after the club. I'll pay for the whole trip. But, we're going to Vegas, not to your friend's thot

party."

Like most of the beautiful black women that Juice had encountered in his lifetime, Bubbles appeared even sexier when she was angry. Her bottom lip poked out in a vicious pout.

Her fingers tightened around the steering wheel. Her nostrils pulsed. There seemed to be a fire under her skin, just out of sight.

"I apologize, baby," Juice said, "and I promise to make it up to you all this weekend. Fuck that, all this *month*. Okay?" He put his left hand on her thigh, squeezed and brushed his thumb over her skin. "You accept my apology?"

That lower lip slowly eased back to its usual position beneath the upper one. The corners of her mouth lifted half an inch. She rolled her eyes and shook her head before she loosened hergrip on the steering wheel.

It amazed Juice how easily Bubbles could get under his skin and warm him up like a quick shot of cognac. He had it bad for her. So bad, in fact, that for the past couple of weeks he hadn't even had the inclination to go on another date. Causal sex had lost its appeal when all he could think about was palming the contours of this stunning brown woman who was soft and curvy, sweet and sexy.

"I'm okay with Vegas," she said. "I've been wanting to go back. Last time I was there only a day. We can grab our toothbrushes and stuff from my place and then head straight to the airport."

"So you accept my apology?"

"I'll accept your apology when I'm sitting on your face in Las Vegas."

"Don't threaten me with a good time," Juice said and then chuckled. "We can get to that before Vegas."

He got a laugh out of her with that remark. A good laugh. So good that she whacked the ball of her hand on the steering wheel. Juice grinned and kissed her on the cheek.

Then minutes later they were on Chicago Avenue pulling up in front of The Visionary Lounge and then driving around to the rear parking lot. There were people everywhere, about ninety percent of them young black men and women. The parking lot was jammed, but not completely. Bubbles found a spot. She parked and Juice phoned Reese. It was 8:50 P.M.

"What up, old man?" Reese answered.

"I'm out here in the parking lot with Bubbles."

"Okay. Shawnna and Dawn just got here. I sent them up to V.I.P. Go to the back door and wait there. I'm about to send Suwu down to let y'all in. You can come straight up to the V.I.P."

"Yup." Juice hung up. "We got V.I.P. action, baby."

"We better have V.I.P. action." Bubbles was eyeing her reflection in the visor mirror, bouncing to whatever beat was playing in her head. "I wanna be out of here by ten. That way we'll be on a plane by twelve or twelve-thirty. I'll order the tickets while we're in here. That cool with you, Grandpa Juice?"

Juice had no objections.

They got out and walked to the door with the big EXIT sign over it, but it was the second door in the middle of the wall ten feet away that was opened for them a moment later. Suwu stepped halfway out and waved to them. "Unc! Wrong door, Unc!"

As Juice followed Bubbles to the half opened door where Suwu stood waving for them, he noticed that there was a large white Mercedes Sprinter van and two long white Cadillac Escalades parked side by side next to the door. A pair of dark-suited Hispanic men were walkingcircles around the vehicles.

Suwu led the way up to the V.I.P. door. "Y'all ain't gon' believe who's all in here," he said. "I couldn't believe it myself."

He opened the door and moved aside for them to enter. Juice crossed thc threshold behind Bubbles and then they stopped. Juice looked around at all of the famous faces and their entourages and then his eyes went back to the famous billionaire couple whose faces had stoppedhim and Bubbles in their tracks. Juice couldn't believe it.

They were in the V.I.P. section with Bulletface and Alexus Costilla.

Chapter 30

Bubbles turned right around and headed back down the stairs. "Fuck this, we're leaving,"she said just as Juice caught up with her and grabbed her elbow. She snatched away and kept going.

Shaking his head defeatedly, Juice gave up on trying to stop her. He glanced back and saw that Reese was descending the stairs with him.

"Damn, what happened?" Reese asked.

"Shit, I don't know," Juice said. "I'll call you. Just watch after the twins and make sure they get home safe."

He grasped her elbow again when they made it to the door. This time she spun around toface him. There were tears in her eyes; big crocodile tears. She dropped her forehead into his chest. He put a hand on her back and gave it an amorous rub.

"It's okay, baby," Juice said in a consoling whisper.

"I'm sorry. I'm sorry." She looked up at him and he thumbed away her tears and kissed her soft lips.

"You don't have to say sorry," Juice said, leaning forward and pressing his lips to her forehead. "If you want to leave we can leave."

Reese came up behind them. "That's my fault. I just thought about it. Bubbles, you and Bulletface used to…mess around. I forgot all about that. Not that I would've had time to tell y'allanyway. He texted me earlier, but I didn't know it was him. Not until he showed up and sent some Mexican dude in to get him and Alexus a spot in V.I.P."

"Let's just go." Bubbles turned her back to Juice and Reese and pushed open the door. The warm night air swept in and she stepped out into that warmth with her head lowered as she sniffled.

Juice went out behind her. The flip-phone vibrated in his pocket. He paid it no mind, choosing instead to look around the parking lot. He would return the call in a little bit. Right nowhe had a bawling girlfriend to look after.

There weren't many people milling around as they had been moments earlier. They were all in line, an African-American centipede easing its way into the nightclub's front door with its back half wrapping around the side of the big building.

Just as Bubbles was settling herself behind the wheel of the silver F-Pace and as Juice was reaching out to open the passenger door, movement to his left caught his attention. He turned his head that way and squinted thoughtfully at a dread-headed young man who had a girl bent over the hood of a dark-colored Camaro. The dread-head was fucking the girl while two other men leaned on the trunk of the Camaro, apparently keeping watch. Or maybe they were waiting to fuck the girl next.

Juice dug the iPhone from his pocket, scrolled down to a number he'd saved as Dead Man, and dialed it while looking leftward at the dread-head as the phone began to ring.

A light blinked on the dread-head's pants which were coiled around his knees. He ignored it.

Even when a jangling ring came from his pants half a second later, he ignored it.

In the F-Pace, Bubbles lowered her forehead against the steering wheel.

Juice felt his heart trip-hammering in his chest. He drew the .45 from his right hip and held itbehind his back as he turned and walked toward the Camaro, dropping the iPhone back into his pocket.

Juice was a pretty good shooter. He had taken a similar weapon to the gun range early last year and practiced his shot.

He whipped the gun around in front of him, held it in both hands, and shot Darren in the side of the head from what must have been teen feet away.

Darren went down like an empty laundry bag. The girl screamed and the two lookouts tried to run away. But they didn't make it far. Juice wasn't taking any chances. He shot one of them in the back and then did the same to the other. Then, he ran up to Darren's grounded figure and pumped three more rounds into the dread-head's skull. With the smoking gun in hand, he ran back to his SUV and climbed in.

"What the fuck just happened?" Bubbles asked. "Nothing," Juice said. "Just drive."

Bubbles shut up and drove and with her NASCAR tendencies, it was an easy getaway.

Chapter 31

It was dark on the plane. Late at night, in the jumbo jet thirty-two thousand feet in the air, most of the passengers in first class were either asleep or watching the glowing screens of their laptops and computer tablets. But, exhausted as Juice and Bubbles were, they could not find it within themselves to surrender to sleep. Instead, theatrically spotlighted by the lights above their seats, they talked in low tones. There was an unconscious need in them both to get to know each other better, especially with the lingering possibility that Juice might soon be arrested.

"I didn't turn around and leave because Blake was there," Bubbles was saying. "Last year, Alexus and some Mexican motherfuckers kicked open my front door and kidnapped me. This was when I lived in New York. They hung me upside down by my ankles in a warehouse. That crazy bitch was going to cut me in half with a chainsaw if Blake hadn't flown in and talked her out of it. I still have nightmares about that day. One on one, I know I'd fuck her up. But she's toorich to fight. She has security for that. Lots of security."

"You'll always be safe with me," Juice promised.

"But what if you get arrested? I'm sure that place has surveillance cameras."

"Reese texted me right before we got on the plane. Everything's good. And if anything doeshappen to me, just move on and live your life."

"Don't say that, Juice. Please. I can't lose you. Not now. Not when I'm just starting to get comfortable with loving you."

"I'll be here, baby." He moved towards her and kissed her passionately. "I ain't goingnowhere."

To Be Continued...
The Brick Man 3
Coming Soon

Lock Down Publications and Ca$h Presents assisted publishing packages.

BASIC PACKAGE $499
Editing
Cover Design
Formatting

UPGRADED PACKAGE $800
Typing
Editing
Cover Design
Formatting

ADVANCE PACKAGE $1,200
Typing
Editing
Cover Design
Formatting
Copyright registration
Proofreading
Upload book to Amazon

LDP SUPREME PACKAGE $1,500
Typing
Editing
Cover Design
Formatting
Copyright registration
Proofreading
Set up Amazon account
Upload book to Amazon
Advertise on LDP Amazon and Facebook page

***Other services available upon request. Additional

charges may apply

Lock Down Publications
P.O. Box 944
Stockbridge, GA 30281-9998
Phone # 470 303-9761

Submission Guideline

Submit the first three chapters of your completed manuscript to ldpsubmissions@gmail.com, subject line: Your book's title. The manuscript must be in a .doc file and sent as an attachment. Document should be in Times New Roman, double spaced and in size 12 font. Also, provide your synopsis and full contact information. If sending multiple submissions, they must each be in a separate email.

Have a story but no way to send it electronically? You can still submit to LDP/Ca$h Presents. Send in the first three chapters, written or typed, of your completed manuscript to:

LDP: Submissions Dept
Po Box 944
Stockbridge, Ga 30281

DO NOT send original manuscript. Must be a duplicate.

Provide your synopsis and a cover letter containing your full contact information.

Thanks for considering LDP and Ca$h Presents.

NEW RELEASES

COKE KINGS 5 by T.J. EDWARDS
MONEY GAME 2 by SMOOVE DOLLA
LOYAL TO THE SOIL by JIBRIL WILLIAMS
A GANGSTA'S PAIN by J-BLUNT
MONEY IN THE GRAVE 2 by MARTELL
"TROUBLESOME" BOLDEN
THE BRICK MAN 2 by KING RIO

Coming Soon from Lock Down Publications/Ca$h Presents

BLOOD OF A BOSS **VI**

SHADOWS OF THE GAME II

TRAP BASTARD II

By **Askari**

LOYAL TO THE GAME **IV**

By **T.J. & Jelissa**

IF TRUE SAVAGE **VIII**

MIDNIGHT CARTEL IV

DOPE BOY MAGIC IV

CITY OF KINGZ III

NIGHTMARE ON SILENT AVE II

By **Chris Green**

BLAST FOR ME **III**

A SAVAGE DOPEBOY III

CUTTHROAT MAFIA III

DUFFLE BAG CARTEL VII

HEARTLESS GOON VI

By **Ghost**

A HUSTLER'S DECEIT III

KILL ZONE II

BAE BELONGS TO ME III

By **Aryanna**

KING OF THE TRAP III

By **T.J. Edwards**

GORILLAZ IN THE BAY V

3X KRAZY III

STRAIGHT BEAST MODE II

De'Kari

KINGPIN KILLAZ IV

STREET KINGS III

PAID IN BLOOD III

CARTEL KILLAZ IV

DOPE GODS III

Hood Rich

SINS OF A HUSTLA II

ASAD

RICH $AVAGE II

MONEY IN THE GRAVE II

By Martell Troublesome Bolden

YAYO V

Bred In The Game 2

S. Allen

CREAM III

By Yolanda Moore

SON OF A DOPE FIEND III

HEAVEN GOT A GHETTO II

By Renta

LOYALTY AIN'T PROMISED III

By Keith Williams

I'M NOTHING WITHOUT HIS LOVE II

SINS OF A THUG II

TO THE THUG I LOVED BEFORE II

By Monet Dragun

QUIET MONEY IV

EXTENDED CLIP III

THUG LIFE IV

By **Trai'Quan**

THE STREETS MADE ME IV

By **Larry D. Wright**

IF YOU CROSS ME ONCE II

By **Anthony Fields**

THE STREETS WILL NEVER CLOSE II

By K'ajji

HARD AND RUTHLESS III

THE BILLIONAIRE BENTLEYS II

Von Diesel

KILLA KOUNTY II

By Khufu

MONEY GAME III

By Smoove Dolla

A GANGSTA'S KARMA II

By FLAME

JACK BOYZ VERSUS DOPE BOYZ

A DOPEBOY'S DREAM III

By Romell Tukes

MURDA WAS THE CASE II

Elijah R. Freeman

THE STREETS NEVER LET GO II

By Robert Baptiste

AN UNFORESEEN LOVE III

By **Meesha**

KING OF THE TRENCHES II
by **GHOST & TRANAY ADAMS**

MONEY MAFIA II

LOYAL TO THE SOIL II

By **Jibril Williams**

QUEEN OF THE ZOO II

By **Black Migo**

THE BRICK MAN III

By King Rio

VICIOUS LOYALTY II

By Kingpen

A GANGSTA'S PAIN II

By J-Blunt

Available Now

RESTRAINING ORDER **I & II**

By **CA$H & Coffee**

LOVE KNOWS NO BOUNDARIES **I II & III**

By **Coffee**

RAISED AS A GOON I, II, III & IV

BRED BY THE SLUMS I, II, III

BLAST FOR ME I & II

ROTTEN TO THE CORE I II III

A BRONX TALE I, II, III

DUFFLE BAG CARTEL I II III IV V VI

HEARTLESS GOON I II III IV V

A SAVAGE DOPEBOY I II

DRUG LORDS I II III

CUTTHROAT MAFIA I II

KING OF THE TRENCHES

By **Ghost**

LAY IT DOWN **I & II**

LAST OF A DYING BREED I II

BLOOD STAINS OF A SHOTTA I & II III

By **Jamaica**

LOYAL TO THE GAME I II III

LIFE OF SIN I, II III

By **TJ & Jelissa**

BLOODY COMMAS I & II

SKI MASK CARTEL I II & III

KING OF NEW YORK I II,III IV V

RISE TO POWER I II III

COKE KINGS I II III IV V

BORN HEARTLESS I II III IV

KING OF THE TRAP I II

By **T.J. Edwards**

IF LOVING HIM IS WRONG…I & II

LOVE ME EVEN WHEN IT HURTS I II III

By **Jelissa**

WHEN THE STREETS CLAP BACK I & II III

THE HEART OF A SAVAGE I II III

MONEY MAFIA

LOYAL TO THE SOIL

By **Jibril Williams**

A DISTINGUISHED THUG STOLE MY HEART I II & III

LOVE SHOULDN'T HURT I II III IV

RENEGADE BOYS I II III IV

PAID IN KARMA I II III

SAVAGE STORMS I II

AN UNFORESEEN LOVE I II

By **Meesha**

A GANGSTER'S CODE I &, II III

A GANGSTER'S SYN I II III

THE SAVAGE LIFE I II III

CHAINED TO THE STREETS I II III

BLOOD ON THE MONEY I II III

A GANGSTA'S PAIN

By J-Blunt

PUSH IT TO THE LIMIT

By **Bre' Hayes**

BLOOD OF A BOSS **I, II, III, IV, V**

SHADOWS OF THE GAME

TRAP BASTARD

By **Askari**

THE STREETS BLEED MURDER **I, II & III**

THE HEART OF A GANGSTA I II& III

By **Jerry Jackson**

CUM FOR ME I II III IV V VI VII

An **LDP Erotica Collaboration**

BRIDE OF A HUSTLA **I II & II**

THE FETTI GIRLS **I, II& III**

CORRUPTED BY A GANGSTA I, II III, IV

BLINDED BY HIS LOVE

THE PRICE YOU PAY FOR LOVE I, II ,III

DOPE GIRL MAGIC I II III

By **Destiny Skai**

WHEN A GOOD GIRL GOES BAD

By **Adrienne**

THE COST OF LOYALTY I II III

By Kweli

A GANGSTER'S REVENGE **I II III & IV**

THE BOSS MAN'S DAUGHTERS I II III IV V

A SAVAGE LOVE **I & II**

BAE BELONGS TO ME I II

A HUSTLER'S DECEIT I, II, III

WHAT BAD BITCHES DO I, II, III

SOUL OF A MONSTER I II III

KILL ZONE

A DOPE BOY'S QUEEN I II III

By **Aryanna**

A KINGPIN'S AMBITON

A KINGPIN'S AMBITION **II**

I MURDER FOR THE DOUGH

By **Ambitious**

TRUE SAVAGE I II III IV V VI VII

DOPE BOY MAGIC I, II, III

MIDNIGHT CARTEL I II III

CITY OF KINGZ I II

NIGHTMARE ON SILENT AVE

By **Chris Green**

A DOPEBOY'S PRAYER

By **Eddie "Wolf" Lee**

THE KING CARTEL **I, II & III**

By **Frank Gresham**

THESE NIGGAS AIN'T LOYAL **I, II & III**

By **Nikki Tee**

GANGSTA SHYT **I II &III**

By **CATO**

THE ULTIMATE BETRAYAL

By **Phoenix**

BOSS'N UP **I , II & III**

By **Royal Nicole**

I LOVE YOU TO DEATH

By **Destiny J**

I RIDE FOR MY HITTA

I STILL RIDE FOR MY HITTA

By **Misty Holt**

LOVE & CHASIN' PAPER

By **Qay Crockett**

TO DIE IN VAIN

SINS OF A HUSTLA

By **ASAD**

BROOKLYN HUSTLAZ

By **Boogsy Morina**

BROOKLYN ON LOCK I & II

By **Sonovia**

GANGSTA CITY

By **Teddy Duke**

A DRUG KING AND HIS DIAMOND I & II III

A DOPEMAN'S RICHES

HER MAN, MINE'S TOO I, II

CASH MONEY HO'S

THE WIFEY I USED TO BE I II

By Nicole Goosby

TRAPHOUSE KING **I II & III**

KINGPIN KILLAZ I II III

STREET KINGS I II

PAID IN BLOOD **I II**

CARTEL KILLAZ I II III

DOPE GODS I II

By **Hood Rich**

LIPSTICK KILLAH **I, II, III**

CRIME OF PASSION I II & III

FRIEND OR FOE I II III

By **Mimi**

STEADY MOBBN' **I, II, III**

THE STREETS STAINED MY SOUL I II

By **Marcellus Allen**

WHO SHOT YA **I, II, III**

SON OF A DOPE FIEND I II

HEAVEN GOT A GHETTO

Renta

GORILLAZ IN THE BAY **I II III IV**

TEARS OF A GANGSTA I II

3X KRAZY I II

STRAIGHT BEAST MODE

DE'KARI

TRIGGADALE I II III

MURDAROBER WAS THE CASE

Elijah R. Freeman

GOD BLESS THE TRAPPERS I, II, III

THESE SCANDALOUS STREETS I, II, III

FEAR MY GANGSTA I, II, III IV, V

THESE STREETS DON'T LOVE NOBODY I, II

BURY ME A G I, II, III, IV, V

A GANGSTA'S EMPIRE I, II, III, IV

THE DOPEMAN'S BODYGAURD I II

THE REALEST KILLAZ I II III

THE LAST OF THE OGS I II III

Tranay Adams

THE STREETS ARE CALLING

Duquie Wilson

MARRIED TO A BOSS I II III

By Destiny Skai & Chris Green

KINGZ OF THE GAME I II III IV V VI

Playa Ray

SLAUGHTER GANG I II III

RUTHLESS HEART I II III

By Willie Slaughter

FUK SHYT

By Blakk Diamond

DON'T F#CK WITH MY HEART I II

By Linnea

ADDICTED TO THE DRAMA I II III

IN THE ARM OF HIS BOSS II

By Jamila

YAYO I II III IV

A SHOOTER'S AMBITION I II

BRED IN THE GAME

By S. Allen

TRAP GOD I II III

RICH $AVAGE

MONEY IN THE GRAVE I II

By Martell Troublesome Bolden

FOREVER GANGSTA

GLOCKS ON SATIN SHEETS I II

By Adrian Dulan

TOE TAGZ I II III

LEVELS TO THIS SHYT I II

By Ah'Million

KINGPIN DREAMS I II III

By Paper Boi Rari

CONFESSIONS OF A GANGSTA I II III IV

By Nicholas Lock

I'M NOTHING WITHOUT HIS LOVE

SINS OF A THUG

TO THE THUG I LOVED BEFORE

By Monet Dragun

CAUGHT UP IN THE LIFE I II III

THE STREETS NEVER LET GO

By Robert Baptiste

NEW TO THE GAME I II III

MONEY, MURDER & MEMORIES I II III

By **Malik D. Rice**

LIFE OF A SAVAGE I II III

A GANGSTA'S QUR'AN I II III

MURDA SEASON I II III

GANGLAND CARTEL I II III

CHI'RAQ GANGSTAS I II III

KILLERS ON ELM STREET I II III

JACK BOYZ N DA BRONX I II III

A DOPEBOY'S DREAM I II

By **Romell Tukes**

LOYALTY AIN'T PROMISED I II

By Keith Williams

QUIET MONEY I II III

THUG LIFE I II III

EXTENDED CLIP I II

By **Trai'Quan**

THE STREETS MADE ME I II III

By **Larry D. Wright**

THE ULTIMATE SACRIFICE I, II, III, IV, V, VI

KHADIFI

IF YOU CROSS ME ONCE

ANGEL I II

IN THE BLINK OF AN EYE

By **Anthony Fields**

THE LIFE OF A HOOD STAR

By Ca$h & Rashia Wilson

THE STREETS WILL NEVER CLOSE

By K'ajji

CREAM I II

By Yolanda Moore

NIGHTMARES OF A HUSTLA I II III

By King Dream

CONCRETE KILLA I II

VICIOUS LOYALTY

By Kingpen

HARD AND RUTHLESS I II

MOB TOWN 251

THE BILLIONAIRE BENTLEYS

By Von Diesel

GHOST MOB

Stilloan Robinson

MOB TIES I II III IV

By SayNoMore

BODYMORE MURDERLAND I II III

By Delmont Player

FOR THE LOVE OF A BOSS

By C. D. Blue

MOBBED UP I II III IV

THE BRICK MAN I II

By King Rio

KILLA KOUNTY

By Khufu

MONEY GAME I II

By Smoove Dolla

A GANGSTA'S KARMA

By FLAME

KING OF THE TRENCHES II

by **GHOST & TRANAY ADAMS**

QUEEN OF THE ZOO

By **Black Migo**

BOOKS BY LDP'S CEO, CA$H

TRUST IN NO MAN

TRUST IN NO MAN 2

TRUST IN NO MAN 3

BONDED BY BLOOD

SHORTY GOT A THUG

THUGS CRY

THUGS CRY 2

THUGS CRY 3

TRUST NO BITCH

TRUST NO BITCH 2

TRUST NO BITCH 3

TIL MY CASKET DROPS

RESTRAINING ORDER

RESTRAINING ORDER 2

IN LOVE WITH A CONVICT

LIFE OF A HOOD STAR

CPSIA information can be obtained
at www.ICGtesting.com
Printed in the USA
LVHW021933190222
711543LV00019B/1770